Rees surveyed the compound; there seemed to be no change in the mission station since he had left three hours ago. Then he tensed. Something was wrong. There was no hum of machinery from the lab—the a-motor wasn't running!

Then the warning hit him; the musky, nauseatingly strong odor of Crocs in a killing rage. It could be that some were near now, or it could be the lingering reminder of a recent visit, or attack.

Crouching low, he began to move towards the lab. On the office threshold he halted. A Croc lay dead at his feet.

The body pinned by darts to the desk inside was his uncle.

EYE OF THE MONSTER

by

ANDRE NORTON

ace books
A Division of Charter Communications Inc.
1120 Avenue of the Americas
New York, N.Y. 10036

EYE OF THE MONSTER

Copyright ©, 1962, by Ace Books, Inc.

EYE OF THE MONSTER

One

Rees Naper opened his eyes. He had come into almost instant consciousness from the night's sleep as he always did. But there was something about his awakening this time, and he lay without any other movement save the raising of eyelids, trying to hear, to sense, to think what was different this morning.

A faint breeze shifted through the sonic net across the window to stir the rustling inner drapery within touching distance. That was it! The sounds, or rather the lack of the right ones for this place and hour. Those he had awakened to hear about the mission for months were missing this morning.

Rees moved swiftly, his hand burrowing into the chink between the foam plasta mattress and the bunk frame, reaching for what he had put there last night after hearing the last urgent warning on the com. Leather, satin smooth and silk supple, curled about his fingers as he pulled out the blaster belt with its holstered weapon. He clasped it to his chest as he rolled off the bunk and went to look through the sonic designed to keep out jungle insect life.

The courtyard of the mission lay open in Ishkur's greenish sunlight. A hoobra hen pecked at a bug, then made a running leap to capture the escaping victim before it took wing. Otherwise that space between the buildings was empty, save for the small creatures that lived in the ornamental flower beds and circular pool.

Rees hurriedly pulled on shirt and the breeches with their attached jungle boots. He was chilled in spite of the day's warmth. You could smell it, sniff it up as surely as if it were the perfume of the violet tipped toofaa reeds out there in the water garden. Trouble—bad! Uncle Milo was wrong, and they were going to have to face up to the result of that error in judgment, that ingrained stubbornness on the part of the head of the mission.

Now with the blaster riding on his hip, Rees glanced over his other emergency preparations; the trail bag he had packed last night. It was too late to hope to get away with more than a survival kit. Again, because of Uncle Milo and his refusal to face facts as they were and not as he decreed them to be.

Rees slapped his palm on the hand lock by the corridor door. In the hall he paused for a long moment, his back against the wall, to listen and smell. Six months as Duggan Vickery's hunting assistant had given him some training with which to face this crisis.

No sound of any the Ishkurians about nor any trace of the distinctive body odor of the natives, so easy to detect when their emotions were aroused. Instead the beckoning scent of Terran coffee. Rees followed that quickly. No Iskhurian would drink coffee. The off-world beverage was rank poison as far as they were concerned and even to smell it upset their insides. Which meant the natives must have cleared out of the mission completely or Dr. Naper would not be brewing a pot now.

Rees sped past three rooms to the door at the end of the hall. The man seated at the table in the room beyond glanced up from the recorder-reader, a faint trace of frown automatically lining the space between his deep-set eyes.

"Good morning, Rees." His tone was precise and, as always, disapproving. Milo Naper and the nephew who shared his quarters shared very little else, neither ideas, emotions nor interests.

"What's going on?" Rees halted by the table. The com unit stood in the corner but its message screen was dark. It was not even turned on. He hurried to flick the button, only to be greeted by a din of static. A mountain storm must be in progress, blanketing out any call from the port at Nagassara.

"We can certainly do without that," Dr. Naper snapped. "Turn it off at once. I do not care to hear any more of this foolish blithering about trouble with the tribes. The utter stupidity of those chair warmers at the port leads one to completely despair of the Forces. If those officers would leave their comfortable quarters once in a while to get out and really learn something about this planet and its people, we'd have no more of this howling about trouble to come when the Patrol pulls out. Trouble to come—faught! I've been on Ishkur for twenty years, and the tribes have always been peaceful and very grateful for what we have been able to do for them."

"What about what happened at Aklanba?" Rees curbed his impatience and exasperation. "And the Patrol's always been here to keep order."

"It has always been my experience that off-world traders cause disturbances. Their greedy grasping for profit can start any number of minor outbreaks, even on peaceful worlds. Aklanba should never have been established that close to the Places of the Old Forest. To permit that was just another typical ill-judged decision of the government, a perfect affront to the High Trees. And doubtless the garbled report we heard about the disturbance there was greatly exaggerated. This fear of an Ishkurian uprising when the Patrol leaves is an evil thing.

"I told Jawin yesterday when he chose to take

himself and his family to Nagassara—the Fermals also—that neither of them need look for any further employment here after they discover how foolish their panic was. In fact, I have dictated to the recorder my condemnation of their desertion at the time. Fifteen years of labor and aid to these jungle tribes can not be cancelled out merely because a few troops are going off-world —as they should have done long since. The Council is only coming to their collective senses at last in breaking up such autocratic bounds of control. I have the highest confidence in the assurances of tranquility given by the High Trees. To send away the Patrol is the first step in righting the wrongs of colonialism."

"There was a burning a month ago, and Ishback, Ishgar and Ishwan, all High Trees, directed it." Rees held tightly to his self control. Uncle Milo accepted wholeheartedly the mission line when it came to administration polices.

Dr. Naper's thin cheeks showed a stain of red. "I will not have such falsehoods repeated in my house! That vicious propaganda of the military is enough to foul the mouth of any man who repeats it. I know Ishgar, he has been educated in our schools at Nagassara. To resort to those vile superstitious practices would be utterly foreign to both his training and his nature. If you cannot forget that asinine indoctrination you had at the academy then please do not attempt to spew out such stuff in public here!"

"Then you will continue to stay, in spite of the warning last night?"

"Stay? Of course I'm staying."

"Did the 'copter return yet?"

"I don't know, nor do I care."

Rees held to his temper with a maximum of control. "What about the Beltz family? And that Salarika trader, Sakfor?" he persisted.

"I am glad to say that Gideon Beltz has not been carried away by this irresponsible hysteria with which we have been deluged for the past few weeks. And what the Salariki do is no concern of the mission."

"None of the natives are here this morning."

"Certainly. And I do not expect to see any for at least three days. This is the First Fast of the Leaves. Which only underlines the crass moronity of those officers in Nagassara. The tribes will be fully occupied with planting rituals for the next ten days. And it would be impossible for Ishkurians to make any hostile moves now, which they surely don't wish to, as you will see. This, Rees, is all the result of that infernal meddling on the part of Survey and the other Services. All this clamor concerning trends and precognition reports—the fiasco will simply discredit such twaddle. You will thank me in years to come, boy, that I was able to make the necessary decision on your behalf before you became a real part of their justly disliked and mistrusted employment."

Rees' lips were a thin line, pressed hard against the teeth. He had learned to swallow a lot in the past three years, but this morning he knew he would have to get away from Uncle Milo in a hurry or he'd say the unforgivable and unforgettable. While he had nothing in common with Dr. Naper, and they did much better apart than together, still he had not been able to leave last night with the Jawins. That would have been standing by with a holstered blaster while his uncle, unarmed, faced the charge of a kaga bull.

He did not share Dr. Naper's belief in the good will of the tribes and their continuing friendship once the Patrol's pacifying strength was removed. And somehow he must get his uncle to see the truth and clear out in time. But he could not do it if they quarreled.

"Where are you going now?" Dr. Naper demanded. "You haven't eaten any breakfast."

"I still have a job, if Vickery didn't pull out," Rees said over his shoulder. "By the looks, I'm late at camp already."

The younger man hurried on into the courtyard. It was true that the First Fast could have drawn the mission people back to their villages. But the feeling of danger, which Rees had had weighing on him since his awakening, quieted his tread now, set his eyes to watching bushes, the shadows in doors and windows.

"Rees!"

He whirled in a half crouch, blaster out and ready. Then with the same speed he thumbled the weapon back in the holster.

"Hey, Rees, you're such a quick draw!" Gordy Beltz materialized from under the low hanging branches of a buppu bush, his face liberally smeared golden with the juice of buppu berries. "You going to the animal camp? Take me 'long, please, Rees! There's nobody to play with and I'm lonesome."

Rees hesitated. Gordy could be a pest at times. But at the moment his small form in the oval of the courtyard did have an oddly forlorn appearance. And it certainly wasn't wise for the small boy to be wandering about by himself today.

"Where's your mother, Gordy?"

"She's got lither fever. Dad gave her a shot and told her to stay in bed. And Ishbi and Ishky never came this morning. Dad gave me a py-ri-ration out of the can for breakfast. Please, Rees, can't I go with you? I want to see all the animals again 'fore Captain Vickery ships them out."

Rees stood with his feet slightly apart, his hand on his hips. "And if I take you—what's the order?"

"Don't touch, don't touch anything. I promise, Rees." Gordy pulled a narrow leaf from the bup-pu bush, spit into its middle, twisted it into a knot which he threw into the pool. "By the Tree Blood I promise."

Kids picked up things and got them surprisingly right, Rees thought fleetingly. Gordy made that oath with the same gestures and intonation a Guardian would use. Sure, kids picked things up, they remembered well, too. Why, he himself could still do the fish dance of the Salariki and he was a year less than Gordy in age when they lifted off that world. But then he'd had special training from the time he was old enough to notice anything, intended to make him absorb points of alien culture. As the son of a Survey officer he was supposed to follow his father into that service.

If only Commander Naper had come back safely from the Volsper run. But he had not and Uncle Milo Naper had turned up relentlessly at the cadet school and jerked Rees out. Well, in spite of his efforts, Uncle Milo hadn't made a mission man out of his nephew, only left him dissatisfied and rootless, unhappy, a constant irritation, in a way, to the dedicated people of an antagonistic way of life.

"All right," he told Gordy now. "Come on." He knew what being lonesome meant, to a great-

er degree than he hoped Gordy would ever real-
ize.

"You aren't going by the main path, Rees?"

"I want to look at the 'copter park."

"The 'copter isn't there. It didn't come back
yet. Rees, what does a red alert mean? They were
sending that on the com when Dad shut it off."

"Some trouble—maybe in Nagassara."

"'Cause the Patrol is leaving? Why'd the Patrol leave, Rees?"

One thing Ress had learned from his father's
training; straight answers and truthful ones were
due children. He tried to simplify this one.

"Ishkur has been a part of the South Sector
Empire. That means a collection of different
worlds under one government. Two years ago the
Council decided that frontier planets, such as
this one, should be allowed to set up their own
ruling states. So they ordered the Patrol to with-
draw by a certain date. And all off-worlders who
thought they might need the protection of the
Patrol were to go then also."

"But the Empire was bad, wasn't it, Rees? Dad
says it was bad. The off-worlders shouldn't rule
Ishkurians."

"Some things were bad. In every form of
government we've used so far, Gordy, there are
bad things. But on some worlds our ways were

18

better than the rule the natives had for themselves before we came."

"Not here, though, Dad says that." Gordy grasped Rees's hand and varied the trot he maintained to match the young man's strides with a series of skipping hops.

"Perhaps—" Rees had reached the landing area. Gordy's report was correct, there was no sign of the 'copter. Yet neither Jawin nor Permal would have left the flyer on robo-control when they disembarked with their families at Nagassara. And so it should have ridden back the guide beam for a landing hours ago. Rees' fingers tightened on Gordy's hand until the boy gave a yelp and tried to pull free.

Vickery had a 'copter, one really larger than the mission's, since he had to transport the caged animals in it. They could pack in the Beltz three, and the two Napers easily in one trip. And perhaps the Captain could argue Uncle Milo into seeing some sense. To Dr. Naper, Rees was a boy, stubbornly wrong-headed, but Uncle Milo would be forced to admit Vickery knew the Ishkurians very well and his advice would mean something.

"What's the matter, Rees? How come we have to hurry so fast?"

Rees had quickened pace until Gordy was running.

"I'm late, and if the guides and hunters have

19

left, the Captain will need me to help feed the animals."

At first the clearing down by the river appeared normal. Except no Ishkurians squatted about checking on capture nets, or charring torkum leaves over the fire before they chewed them. The cages ready for transport were arranged around three sides of a hollow square, with the river to the west. But at second glance Rees saw that those cages doors were now swinging wide open, their occupants had all been loosed.

He ran to the plasta bubble of Vickery's tent, pulled open the zip-close. The owner, his guns, his jump bag were all missing. Vickery had cleared out and in a hurry.

Rees fairly leaped past the line of cages to the clearing of the 'copter. Pulled to one side was the jungle roller car, but the flyer was gone.

"Rees," Gordy had followed him into the tent, now he came running with a folded paper in his hand. "This had your name on it. Where's Captain Vickery and all the animals?"

"Gone away." He grabbed the paper from Gordy.

"Notice from the port." The words were hurriedly scrawled. "No ship-off possible for the animals. Red alert, I have to answer militia call. Can't find Kassa, when she turns up, keep her for me, bring her in with you."

Rees swallowed. Kassa! Vickery had not delayed to hunt Kassa! He felt cold all through his middle, sick and cold. Kassa, the Spician hound, was Vickery's prized tracker. The hunter would not have left her except to obey the most urgent order. The off-world militia must have been called up to answer some trouble at the port.

"Gordy!" he called harshly to the boy who had wandered toward the river, "come here!"

"Rees—I can hear something! Please—come and listen!"

But Rees could hear it also, a low throb of whimper, a noise which added to the sick feeling inside him. Suppose—suppose Vickery had not lifted with the 'copter after all? Suppose what had happened at Aklanba had also chanced here? Rees swallowed down growing sick panic.

He caught Gordy's shoulder, propelled the boy to the jungle roller. Pushing him into the seat Rees climbed in also to make a check. Vickery had not even waited to dismantle the sonic screen or dismount the flamer.

"Sit still now!" Ress ordered, caught a glimpse of growing fright on the small face turned toward him. He set his boot heel down on the floor button and the machine came to life.

They smashed straight through a corner of the cage compound, moving to parallel the river. But they did not have far to go. At first Rees was so overjoyed to discover that he had not found Vickery, that he actually drew a deep breath of relief. Until Gordy's cry of horror aroused him to action and he used the blaster on the tortured creature still feebly struggling. That could not have been there long. If it had been in place before Vickery pulled out the Captain would have flamed the whole jungle apart to get even with Kassa's tormentors. Was it meant to be a warning or was it a signal of victory over one off-worlder, and that one a long-time friend?

Gordy was crying now, noisily as might an ordinary small Terran boy, but with dreadful sobs which shook his body. Both of his fists were locked on the fabric of Rees' shirt.

"It's all right!" Rees flung one arm about that shivering body, pulled the child closer. "It's all right now, Gordy." But it was not all right and nothing could make it so. Not now. He shouldn't have brought the child here, but neither could he have left him alone. Somewhere, out in the jungle, eyes watched, Rees was sure of that.

He kicked the roller into action again. Uncle Milo would have to listen to reason now. They could dismount the flamer from this machine, turn the main building of the mission into a fort, appeal by com for rescue. Rees' mind skipped feverishly from one part of a workable plan to the next.

22

Captain Vickery had stood very well, to all outward show, with the natives. He had drunk leaf beer with two local chiefs and witnessed the Felling Dances. You could not say that barbarity was visited on Kassa for any sin of his master. This was no matter of a trading station set up on the border of forbidden territory. This was here and now, an icy warning to every off-worlder in the immediate countryside.

What about the Salariki? Dr. Naper knew nothing about them. Had they been able to go last night? With the machine still turning around at his guidance, Rees hesitated. To cut down by their post would take more time. On the other hand, to leave the Salariki there unwarned was unthinkable.

Their felinoid ancestry did not make them any less "men" at a time such as this and he knew that Sakfor had women and children of his species with him. Rees made a full turn and jammed the speed of the roller up the scale. It took to the air in one of the ground covering bounds which exhausted far too much of its fuel charge but which cut minutes to seconds. The Salariki station and then the mission—and he could only pray that time would not run out for them all!

Two

As were the buildings of the mission, the trading post was constructed of glegg stone blocks, cut, while the substance was still workable, in an excavation on the river bank, put then together to harden under wind and rain into metallic toughness. Short of a force flash such walls could not be razed. But that oily yellow smoke curling up into the sky, the throat catching scent of burning oganna, told Rees now that Sakfor's fort had not been a refuge. His season's gatherings were afire.

Rees slammed the lever on the controls. With a tooth-rocking force the roller halted behind a screen of bush through which the Terran could see the post set in a curve of river bank. There was activity there. Rees' hand flailed out, knocking Gordy off the seat of the machine, down where the boy could no longer view what was happening. For a moment the young man's fingers rested on the firing trigger of the flamer. But they were too far away to catch the looters in its beam. And to betray his own presence there would no longer help the Salariki.

The Terran kicked the reverse, glad that the purr of the sonic screen drowned out most the sounds. The reality of the massacre now ending there was worse than any description broadcast by com. Rees fought the revolt of his stomach as he edged the roller away from that hell which had been a peaceful trading post.

Something flashed away from the forward thrust of the machine as they turned about. Twany yellow. That was no animal! Rees' jungle trained eyes registered its difference and he pulled up quickly, thumbed off the sonic.

But there was no chance of hailing what he believed he had seen. The terrible cries from the post, muffed as they were, still rang! And his own call might bring lurking Ishkurian scouts down upon them. There was a low bush shaking to the right, the fugitive might be sheltering under it. Rees drew Gordy up to face him.

"Listen," he looked directly into the boy's eyes, "this is important, Gordy. Over there, under that bush, I think one of the Salariki children is hiding. If I go over I may frighten it into running. Do you think you can crawl in and bring it out?"

"Rees, what's happening? Rees, that noise—" Gordy shivered in the young man's grasp, his small face registering shock and fright.

"Gordy, that bush over there." Rees shook the boy gently. They could not leave any survivor of the post. And for him to beat the bushes would only drive the terrorized alien child deeper into hiding. Gordy was the only way to locate the Salariki cubling.

Gently Rees turned the boy around, pointed to the bush. Then he shook Gordy again, thankful to see a measure of comprehension dawn in the child's face. With drawn blaster in one hand and the other on Gordy's shoulder, Rees eased them both out of the roller and towards the bush. Still some feet away from the objective he released his hold on the boy, gave him a push in the right direction. Mercifully that yammering screaming had stopped. What they heard now was only the blatting of the natives.

Gordy went to his hands and knees, crawled under the dropping branches of the shrub. There was an agitated shaking and Gordy's plump buttocks, his scuffed boots reappeared. He was retreating backwards, tugging at some recalcitrant captive, both hands clasped about two small wrists while fingers with claw nails writhed for freedom.

Rees made a swift swoop, felt the rake of those nails, cruel and sharp across his cheek and chin as he gathered a spitting, wildly threshing small body up in his arms. Gordy, without being told, was already streaking back to the safety of the roller. And Rees followed, to put his fright-maddened captive down in the seat between them. He fended those raking nails with his forearm while he activated the sonic and set the roller on its way again. Only then, when they were in motion, did he take a closer look at the rescued.

She crouched all together, her point-tip ears flattened against her rounded skull, her mouth half open as she hissed silently in the heritage of her long ago feline ancestors. The fine, plushy, fur-hair on her head and along her backbone and outer arms was roughened and standing erect. Her orange-red eyes, set aslant in her broad face, were slitted and wild.

Rees had no way of determining Salariki ages. She might have been younger than Gordy or older. Her torn garment was a short kilt held about her waist by a jeweled belt from which still hung a few scent bags suspended on beautifully patterned ribbons. The ribbons for others were torn and fluttering free. So, by her dress, she was still a young child, and a favored one, probably one of Sakfor's daughters. Salariki females did not circulate freely except among their own people, and Rees had no idea of the number or ages of those composing Sakfor's late household. The Terran did know that a man of influence living off the Salariki home planet was allowed more than one wife, usually marrying two or three sisters from the same family clan.

The Salarika's head turned slowly as she surveyed Gordy, Rees, and the interior of the roller.

A red, sharply pointed tongue licked out across her face and flipped in between her teeth again.

"She's got fur on her." Gordy put out an investigating finger but he did not quite touch the soft golden down covering the outer side of the arm next to him. "She sure smells nice, doesn't she?" His nose wrinkled as the heavy scents from those waist bags grew stronger in the machine. Apparently he was so interested in the newcomer he had forgotten the sights and sounds of the immediate past. Rees nodded.

"Salariki people love perfumes, Gordy. Those are their principal trade items." He could have bitten out his tongue at that slip but Gordy had not apparently noticed.

"What's her name, Rees?" the boy continued.

"I don't know," the young man was more occupied with finding a way through the mass ahead. To keep the machine to any open path was to invite immediate discovery. And what had happened at the mission? Had his decision been the wrong one? Had he thrown away the lives of three Terrans when he had chosen to go fruitlessly to the post? Sweat beaded Rees' face, rolled in glistening drops down to salt his lips and drip from his chin.

"What's your name?" Gordy asked in Basic. "I'm Gordy Beltz. I live at the mission."

The Salarika licked her face again and then

raised one hand. Blood oozed from between two of her fingers. She applied her tongue there also.

"Rees, she's hurt! Her fingers're all bloody!"

Rees glanced sidewise. "A bad scratch, Gordy. But it's stopped bleeding. I'll see to it as soon as I can." He hoped that the Salariki followed the usual off-world custom and innoculated their kind against alien diseases. But he must reach the mission, he must.

"We're almost home," Gordy announced a short time later. "I see the big crook-tree. Mom, she'll give you something for your finger," he assured the Salarika. "Does it hurt much?"

Those almost noiseless hisses no longer issued from the alien. Her examination of her companions continued, but her hair was no longer standing erect and she appeared to be settling down. Rees doubted if she understood Basic. But he believed she had sensed the good will of the Terrans and their difference from those devils back at the post.

"Rees, what are you stopping here for? Why don't you drive down the road?" Gordy's questions were strung together. His face was paling once more as the young man pulled the machine to a stop well away from the mission buildings.

Rees dared not drive in until he knew conditions ahead. It would be better to avoid the usual approach and take a more concealed way from

30

the copse of farb trees. Those would screen any scouting expedition clear to the laboratory building.

"Rees, Dad's going to be awful mad at you, running this roller across a planted field, he had doman seeds put in here last week." Gordy's hands clenched on the edge of the instrument board. "Please, Rees, what's the matter?" His momentary interest in the Salarika forgotten, he was beginning to shiver once more.

"Gordy, be quiet!" Rees maneuvered the roller along, trying to keep it screened from any enemy that might lurk about the mission. He thought he could get the machine well in unseen. Of course, so far he had seen no sign that the natives had been here. But they might well infest the jungle, be closing in about the clearing ready for an attack.

Rees brought the jungle car to a halt and turned in the seat to face both children.

"Now listen, Gordy, this is very important. We have to get your Dad, your mother, and my Uncle Milo, take them away from here or else gather them in one place where we can fight. Do you understand that?"

Gordy's hands were knuckle-white in that grip on the edge of the panel. But his nod told the young man that he was taking this all in.

"You are to stay here, in the roller with the Salarika. She's afraid and if she's left alone she may try to run away again. Then we might lose her in the jungle. So I'm trusting you to see she stays here, Gordy."

"While you go to get Mom and Dad, Rees?"

"Yes. And if there are native hiding around here they mustn't see us so don't leave this machine!"

"You can send a message on the com, then the Patrol will come and take us away," Gordy's hold on the panel eased.

"Yes, we'll do something like that. But you stay right here with the Salarika, Gordy. I'll be back as soon as I can. Now see this button? It controls the sonic. I have to turn that off when I get out. You press it down to put the curtain back up again. And keep it up all the time I'm gone."

Gordy nodded solemnly. Rees hoped he would follow orders. With that sonic up the children had a measure of protection. It reacted against Ishkurian ears in a painful manner—but that was scanty enough.

"I'm going now. And Gordy, even if Ishbi or Ishky come—don't go to them." Rees had no way of knowing if the mission natives were among the raiders, but he dared take no chances that they were still friendly.

"Yes, Rees."

The young man got out, watched Gordy thumb

on the sonic, and then sprinted for the side of the nearest building. The cloying scent which had filled the interior of the roller, rising from the Salarika's clothing, began to clear from his nostrils. He stood braced against the rough wall for a long moment, using both ears and nose to give him warning of trouble.

Only the chirrup of insects, the bubbling call of the hoobra hens, the sigh of breeze through shrubbery, all peaceful sounds. But no welcoming hum from the laboratory—the a-motor was not running. And Rees tensed. He slipped along the wall, no windows broke its surface here, he would have to go around to the courtyard side before he could really see anything of the mission's interior.

At this hour Beltz should be in the lab, and Rees' uncle either there or in the house. Gordy said his mother was sleeping off one of the fever attacks. Three people to locate and warn. Mrs. Beltz first? Or the men in the lab? But they would have screens up there; a small protection but still enough to give them warning. The woman was alone; Again Rees must choose.

He was still against the wall, masked by one of the bushes. As far as he could see from here there had been no change in the garden courtyard since he had crossed it more than three hours ago.

Then the warning hit him full force, carried

by a puff of wind ruffling the long spikes of leaves about him; the reek of native body odor, musky, nauseatingly strong. That was the smell of a Croc who was heated, excited. *Croc*—a forbidden epithet here, but one Rees knew. Croc stink here, and strong!

The Terran studied the peaceful scene, trying to guess at the source of that stench. It could be that one of those horny bodies crouched very close to him now. Or the smell could be only a lingering reminder of the recent visit of an Ishkurian aroused to the fever pitch of some strong emotion.

To reach the Beltz cottage, he would have to keep between hedge and lab wall, past the storeroom, hidden most of the way. Crouching low Rees began the ordeal of that venture. So far his nose could not pin the Croc smell to any one section. And he had seen no disturbance in the courtyard. His training in hunting craft, all he had learned during those months with Vickery, would now be put to the test.

Rees scuttled from one clump of lace-thong to the next. Then his hand went to the sill of the window which must open on the Belt' sleeping room. To go around to the door meant advancing into plain sight. And he could endure the pain of passing through a sonic long enough to get in.

Cara Beltz should still be sleeping after that shot. He would have to rouse her.

He was head and shoulders over the sill and then he lurched back. The Croc reek was a deadly miasma in that room. He did not need more than one sickened glance at the bed to know what had happened. Stomach heaving, Rees crouched back into the bushes, using the control he had been taught at the academy to master his body so it would not betray him by sounds of retching. At least she must have been still asleep when they got to her and probably never knew. He could cling to that hope.

There was no reason to try the lab now. The absence of motor hum was only too well explained. What about the com? Could he summon help by that? But that warning last night had been firm and final. You had to reach the port by 'copter then—and on your own. No rescue missions to be flown. And their 'copter had not returned. As for the one at the trading post, the Crocs would have destroyed that, they weren't stupid.

However, in the house were other things which could mean life for fugitives. His own trail bag and its contents—he must make a try for that. Rees mastered the involuntary shaking of his body, studied the courtyard once more while he mapped out his next movements.

He did not make those until he had decided just what and where he must go. Then he went into action with swift sureness to reach another window, that of his own room.

Crocs had been here all right. Rees' took in the incredible confusion of the looted room, the paw marks and scratches where they had tried to force palm locks of the cupboards. But Ishkurian body heat was radically different from Terran. They had not been able to activate those controls. Short of chopping down the walls the storage cupboards were safe.

Rees pressed his hand over one of those smears, his flesh shrinking from even such a remote contact with the murderers. From the now open cupboard he snatched the bag he had packed so carefully and he gathered up three spider silk blankets too, as well as the long bladed dagger which had been one of his father's gifts. Good as dura-steel was, it could not penetrate Croc hide, but there was other life besides the natives to be met in the jungle. And the jungle would have to be their refuge.

Opening one of the blankets Rees dumped all his gatherings into that and knotted the whole into an unwieldly bag which he hurled out of the window. Outside again he stood above his loot to listen and sniff.

Why the Crocs had struck and then gone so

soon puzzled him. There had been no fires here, no evidence that they had amused themselves after the beastly fashion they had at the post. A quick kill of the Terrans, then a fade away. Why?

Sakfor's post had been a relatively primitive structure, his storehouses easily raided. The mission was a more complex system of lab, warehouse, living quarters. Had the Ishkurians perhaps been afraid of the lab and its equipment? Or did they intend to return at their leisure for a more prolonged looting?

The natives working at the mission whom Dr. Naper had promoted to tasks about the lab did have some elemental technical training. Those three at least knew the value and the use of much of the equipment. And there were things in the lab which could be turned into far more formidable weapons than the dart guns and throw ropes of the jungle people.

Rees did not know why he thought about that now. But it stuck tight in his mind, a kind of "hunch". And in the Academy hadn't they always stressed the value of examining the basis of such a hunch? Somebody might have wanted the mission left intact, somebody might be able to turn off-world machines, off-world ideas against the off-worlders who had imported them. He must remember that, and he prepared to face just such a problem.

But there was nothing he could do here to wreck the installations. In fact, the two Ishkurian technicians knew more about what was in the lab than Rees did. And he had to get back to the roller before it attracted any attention.

Gordy saw him coming and snapped off sonic. Slinging his bundle back into the storage space. Rees settled himself once more behind the controls.

"Where's Mom?"

Rees flinched as much from that question as from the touch of Gordy's hand on his arm.

"She's gone, Gordy, so has your Dad, and Dr. Naper."

"Where? But Mom wouldn't go without me!" Gordy's protest was sharp, fear-filled.

"She was sick, remember, Gordy. She must have been sleeping when they left. We're going on to the big plantation by the mountains, maybe we'll meet the 'copter and them there."

Rees could not bring himself to tell Gordy the truth, not there and then with Gordy's own memories of Kassa and the trading post still raw and horrible. And he had to think ahead further than just a few minutes, or an hour. The post, Vickery's hunting camp where he had been gathering the animals sold to off-world zoos, the mission; as far as Rees knew those were the only off-world holdings this far west.

The proxlite mines had closed down two months ago when the first broadcast had suggested off-world withdrawal. But between them now and the mountains, the range which sealed away the plain and the Nagassara space port, there were two plantations. One of them, Wrexul's, was large enough to maintain its own private police force. If the fugitives could reach that and the off-world staff had not already left—A black collection of "ifs" but that was all Rees had to hold to.

The immediate problem was to find some place to hole up until dark came. In the night he would dare to use hopping power and really make speed. To keep to the jungle floor was to leave a trail a half-blind, jungle-foolish tourist could follow. And to hop in daylight was as revealing. Yes, a hiding hole for now; and after dark run east for Wrexul's!

Three

The roller was concealed between two points of rocks, crouching as might a spurred yandu in a tree den. Rees had driven back along that camp trail which numerous hunting expeditions had beated down, and then lifted the machine by one carefully timed hop into this pocket. Lace thongs made a protecting gray-green curtain about them when he had pulled those elastic branches into position, following a pattern which Vickery had early taught him during their trapping. He plunged in the sense alarm making them safe from any surprise attack. And, with a stone wall behind them, the flamer facing the only entrance way, they were in the best fort he could improvise.

Rees looked at his watch. Four hours and a little more since he had left Uncle Milo at the breakfast table. Four hours, enough time to end a world.

"Rees, I'm thirsty." Gordy tugged at his sleeve.

Water? Food? There were always survival rations stored in the roller. But how was the water? To check the tank had been one of the first morning jobs, he had had other things to think about today.

Rees knelt on the seat to read the gauge. About half full, which meant they must use that supply sparingly. But there were other ways of obtaining water in the jungle and they should keep the contents of the tank for emergencies.

"I want a drink!" Gordy persisted.

"I'll get you one. You stay here, turn on the sonic again after I get out but stay inside, understand?"

The young man worked one of the plastic canteens out of its hold hook and tucked the jungle knife into his belt. Both the Salarika and Gordy watched his preparations with round-eyed interest.

He slid out of the roller, wiggled between two of the lace thongs, and then paused, to listen and sniff. What he sought should be found not too far away. Rees rounded one of the protecting rock piers and plunged into the misty, gray-green of the jungle world, his boots sinking inches deep into the powdery earth.

A ghost-wing fluttered by, its pale, almost completely transparent wings making it seem the shadow of the living creature which no Terran had yet been able to classify either as a bird or an over-large insect. Rees stood statue still to check that flight. And he was rewarded when the ghost-

42

wing settled on a bulbaceous growth swelling a loop of vine about the rough trunk of a thorn-rump.

That would be on a thorn-rump, Rees thought ruefully, measuring the distance between the ground and the vine by eye and guess. Luckily the tree was old and so there was a goodly stretch of open space between the dark purple thorns. He could climb, though it was a chance he would not ordinarily take. Setting the knife blade between his teeth and thrusting the canteen into the front of his shirt, Rees gingerly took finger hold on the threatening thorns, pulled himself up until he could hook one hand over the vine near that promising swelling.

Seen this close the growth was not a part of the vine, but a parasite rooted on it, globular, with a fantastic spread of hairlike purple foliage sprouting from its lower end. The ghost-wing emerged from among those waving fronds, fluttering out in panic. Rees made a one hand stab with the knife into the side of the globe. The purple filaments writhed up and about his wrist. But he had braced himself in advance for their scratching and he knew he was immune to the particular poison they dug into his skin.

Restoring his knife to teeth grip again, Rees now pressed the mouth of the canteen tight to the hole he had made in the globe, boring in with all the strength he could exert. The bulb shrank under that pressure and the purple threads hung limp about an emptied husk, the liquid contents of which now splashed in the canteen. Rees dropped back to the floor of the jungle, a good supply of drinkable water now in hand.

His return was a backward crawl, for as he went he erased with a branch the marks of his boots. Luckily the powdery soil was easily smoothed. Then he was again in the roller with the eager children. As he let them drink the Terran wondered about the Salarika's immunity. Gordy was safe against jungle virus and the results of most insect bites. But was this small alien also protected by some form of inoculation or mutant control? They would have to chance it that she was.

She drank thirstily enough and he tried again to talk to her in Basic. Though she watched him with close attention, she did not answer, and he thought that if she did understand his words perhaps she could not speak that common stellar tongue.

However she allowed Rees to examine her torn hand. The blood had been licked away and the scratch looked clean. When the Terran tried to cover it with a plastic band, she shook her head violently and pulled away, licking at it again with her tongue in a methodical up and down fashion.

Rees guessed she was following her own species' way of dealing with such hurts. It was better for him not to interfere, what served one people did not always aid another.

"Why are we staying here, Rees?" Gordy demanded. "If Mom and Dad are waiting with the 'copter by the mountains I want to go on now!"

"We can't go until dark," Rees returned, summoning patience. To stay cooped up in the roller for the rest of the day would be hard on Gordy, probably on the Salarika child, too. But they dared not leave its safety. How frank could he be with the boy? Rees' own father had treated him as an adult, but then he had been Survey.

When his mother had died Rees had been only a little older than Gordy was now, but already the veteran of two prelim settlements on newly discovered planets. And he had continued to accompany his father as a matter of course, that life was a part of Survey training, until, at the age of twelve, he had mustered in at the Academy.

Specialization in service families had reached the point that children were born into their fathers' and mothers' occupations. That was why the wrench had come as a major break for Rees when Dr. Naper had taken him from the Academy and tried to refit him into the mission pattern of life. He could not subscribe to Uncle Milo's abhorrence of Survey's basic tenets. Just as he could not and would not agree that Survey's opening of new planets only tended to increase the colonial rule of the Empire and perpetuate what Dr. Naper and those of his association considered the most pernicious aspect of Terran galactic expansion.

But Gordy was of a mission family and relatively far less tough and less prepared for just what had happened today. Was he still young enough to be elastic, or would memory re-hab be his lot if and when they escaped?

"If we move now the Crocs might find us." Rees tried to explain.

"You mustn't call them 'Crocs'," Gordy corrected him. "That's a degrade name."

A degrade name! There it was, mission conditioning. Rees frowned impatiently. He'd like to force the mission high echelon personnel to sit through a tape film of what had happened here three hours ago. Sure, any one with a fraction of good sense did not intentionally degrade any intelligent alien race. But neither was it right to disregard the fact that in dealing with aliens, Terran, or even humanoid standards could not remain the measuring sticks of judgement. On the side of the mission there had been such a determined indoctrination away from normal human wariness in dealing with X-tees that to question any "native" motives was close to a venial sin.

Rees supposed that what had just happened here would be explained and excused by those policy makers in a way to satisfy everyone but the dead, the tortured dead.

"The natives," Rees corrected. "Gordy, this is important—the natives don't like us any more. If they see us—they'll kill."

"Like what the Patrol officer said on the com?"

"Just as he said on the com," Rees confirmed.

"I want Mom and Dad!" Gordy's lower lip protruded stubbornly, now it quivered.

"Well, they aren't here!" Rees' exasperation grew. He knew that this had been a day of shocks for the boy, but the mere fact that they were still alive meant something. Though, he corrected himself silently, Gordy had no way of recognizing that.

"Tonight we'll turn on the hopper, head for Wrexul's plantation. Now let me switch on the hummer and you and the Salarika curl up back there and see if you can sleep."

"Travel at night," Gordy considered the possibilities that offered. "Stay up all night and maybe see an air dragon, Rees?"

"Truly. But you won't be able to see any air dragon unless you get sleep enough so you *can* stay awake tonight." Rees accepted the diversion gratefully.

He spread out two of the blankets on the floor

of the storage compartment, gave each of the children another drink, set the small hummer, once used to quiet newly captured animals, to lull them to sleep, pleased that the girl seemed content to follow Gordy's example. Then Rees settled himself down in a corner of the driver's seat, on his knee the recorder which was one remainder from the good life with his father.

Commander Tait Naper had never been on Ishkur. But he had had training in handling widely varied alien beings. And his private note tapes, left behind when he had taken off on that last voyage, were a rich inheritance for his son. They held distilled experience hints from his successful career. Rees thumbed the button now, though the key words for his own need: jungle, hostiles, escape, and waited for the re-run beam to reach his mind.

Fifteen minutes later he snapped off the recorder. None of the specific information the beam had planted in his mind was closely applicable to the here and now. But a general idea or two . . .

"Eye of the spider," he repeated softly aloud. "If you would fight a spider, you must attempt to see through its eyes, think with its mental equipment, foresee its attack as it would make one.'"

The spiders in this case were the Crocs and

Rees would have to strive to think Croc in order to out-think Croc, a rather confused estimate of the task, but a correct one.

What did he know about the Crocs, the educated ones at the mission, the servile class that did the heavy labor, the guides and hunters with whom he had worked in Vickery's camp? These were three types, reacting in three separate ways. You could tongue-click and clapper Croc speech, the audible speech. But no off-worlder could mind-touch as it was certified that Crocs did with one another.

Yes, you could learn something of the outward forms of Croc life: the fisherfolk of the sea shore, the hunters of the jungle, the handful of those who had chosen to learn something of off-world education and galactic civilization. But you did not really know what went on in those sloping, reptilian skulls. To use the eye of the spider here —the task was close to impossible. But Survey never accepted the term impossible.

Rees closed his eyes, tried to evaluate as he had been taught; if he had only had more training! He was in the position of a man ordered to build a spacer, with a full list of materials to draw upon, and only a beginner's knowledge of engineering. His concentration became close to physical pain as he forced himself to study the problems of getting under a rough, armor plated skin, seeing through the "eye of the spider," trying to foresee the moves of the Crocs against the fugitives.

Again it was the absence of sound which alerted Rees, as it had when he had awakened hours earlier that morning. The sonic! His hand was already reaching for the proper button on the control panel. Could the roller power unit be failing?

But as his finger rammed home on the button, that faint vibration began again. No power failure, a turn-off. Gordy! Rees hunched around to peer into the storage compartment behind the driver's seat. But Gordy was there, stretched out full length, short arms and legs flung wide. Gordy was there—the Salarika child was gone!

How had she known? But then she'd watched Gordy turn the sonic on and off. Why had she gone; after food, water? Rees had fed the children, and the half full canteen was within easy reach. No, the canteen was gone, as was a fish spear which had lain along the back of the storage space—water, a weapon of sorts. Their fugitive from the post must be following some definite course of action. Was she going back, trying to find others of her family? That was far more probable than the idea a child would strike into the jungle for any other reason.

Rees rubbed his hands across his forehead. She

couldn't have been gone very long. The breaking of the sonic had alerted him. How much of a homing instinct had her feline ancestors bequeathed her? Enough to guide her through the miles of jungle to the post? Not that she could make such a journey. The jungle was safe only when traveled by a hunter; any off-worlder must go in a machine equipped with the ingenious multitude of detective and protective devices this one possessed.

But how could he hunt down a small Salarika who probably was determined against being found, with a thousand good hiding places to hand? There was only one answer, and it was a danger for all of them—the roller must be used. The sense detector in it could be used to nose out any living thing with intelligence about a set quotient. Rees had it connected now as a Croc warning but it could as easily put him on the trail of the Salarika.

He leaned forward to study the dial. That was set to register at the mark Vickery had put there months previously, reporting on Croc mental radiations, meant to keep track of foot hunters on a drive. What would Salariki thought beams be? Closer to human, Rees guessed. The Crocs were a reptilian species; Salarika were mammals, warm-blooded and off-world. He moved the pointer with infinite care and then his heart beat faster with excitement. A tiny spark of answer. He could use the tracer though that meant hunting with the machine.

Rees activated the motor, his eyes moving quickly from what lay ahead to the tracer dial. The spark fluttered faster, then settled to a steady dot of fire. He was on course. The path weaved away from the rock pillars, heading on the slight down slope. That was a direct route back for the post. If they only had a common language and he had been able to explain the danger. He could now believe that the cubling was certain she had been virtually kidnapped, taken by force from her own kind. Perhaps, as a female, she had had so little contact with off-worlders of other species that she associated Rees and Gordy with the raiding Crocs!

Now that the Terran was sure of the direction of her trail he could try something else. Rees set the prowler to hop, cleared a large path of vegetation and settled down in the midst of a stream where water circled about the treads. They were ahead of the fugitive now, instead of trailing. And she would come to them.

Only she did not. Rees' frown grew. The spark on the dial remained constant. The Salarika was making no move. Had she witnessed their hop, was she remaining hidden to wait out the hunt? Well, he dared not waste the time in such games.

This called again for Gordy's aid. Rees snapped off the hummer, reached back to shake the boy awake.

It required a moment or two to make Gordy understand. And when he did, he stared up the slope where the bush was thick and shook his head dubiously.

"I don't see, Rees, how we can find her there. There are so many places she can hide."

"Our noses will have to do it for us." Rees stepped out of the roller, almost knee deep into the water, and then swung Gordy from the machine to the up slope bank. "She's still wearing those perfume bags. Here, sniff this!" He had dosed himself with the inhaling powder which made him sneeze and had an even more violent effect on the boy.

"That hurts!" Gordy complained, rubbing his nose vigorously with the back of a grimy hand.

"Only for a minute," Rees assured him. "Take some deep breaths, Gordy." The inhalant had only a temporary effect and it could not be used again for hours. But the perfume of the Salariki clothing should be easy to pick up when their sense of smell was so intensified.

They started up the slope together, Gordy still rubbing his smarting nose. Suddenly he looked up at his tall companion. "I can smell, lots of things—different things!"

The sense of smell, so blunted in his species during their evolvement on their own world, was probably not yet as keen as that of an average animal, but it was far more effective than usual. And they were favored because the breeze was towards them—down hill. The wind must pass over whereever their quarry was in hiding.

"Over here!" Gordy jumped to the right, skidded down on one knee and scrambled up again. Rees moved to join him.

The boy was right. That scent which had hung about them so heavily in the roller was on the down breeze. They could not be too far away. But there was something else, a reek that was no perfume. *Croc!* grabbed for Gordy.

He held the boy fast as he drew a deep questing breath. Salariki and Croc all right. But the Croc stench was old, certainly nothing as strong as the taint left at the mission. An excited Croc had been there, but was no longer lurking nearby. Rees released Gordy but the boy did not move away.

"I smell . . ." he began and Rees nodded.

"Yes, but it's old, maybe since yesterday. Come on."

Rees broke through a stand of bushes, to face a dark hole in the ground. He cried out and threw himself flat, to wriggle forward and look down into a trail trap dug for one of the large beasts the jungle natives considered the best of eating.

The pit was dark, only a small portion of its covering had broken under the slight weight of the Salarika girl. Rees wondered if she had jumped from above to the seemingly secure surface of this place and her landing had snapped the roofing of the trap.

She was inside right enough, on her feet, her back against the wall, her forearm streaming blood where the flesh had scraped a upward pointing stake set to impale a captive. Mercifully she had escaped with only that hurt. Her yellow eyes were alight in the dark as she looked up at him, voicing a faint wordless plaint.

"Gordy!" Rees turned his head as he edged back from that danger section. The Crocs always undermined the edges of such a pit against any escape efforts. His own weight here might bring about another slip which would entrap them all, hold them prisoners for the Croc hunter. Gordy would have to act as his tool now.

"Is she down there?"

Rees nodded as he slashed and dug at the roots of the bushes about the hole. Those were long and tough, pulled up fairly easy when the fastening tendrils were loosened. They would make a rope of sorts and Gordy must do the rest under Rees' direction.

Four

Rees worked fast. With the root lengths freed from the soil, he jerked and tore off the smaller side tendrils until he had a length of reasonably supple line, tough enough to stand the strain of Gordy's weight. He explained carefully to the boy what must be done, made him tie by himself twice over the necessary knots. To Rees' relief, Gordy was an apt pupil, appeared to understand just what he must do and why.

Then, with one end of the root rope tied about his middle, Gordy crawled out to the break and dropped into the pit. As Rees had feared the saw action of the root cord on the brink of that drop sent another portion of the concealing covering cascading down into the pit below. But Gordy swung free well above the danger of the stakes.

Rees looped the rope about a sapling, lowered it hand over hand until Gordy hailed that he had reached the bottom. The rope went slack. Gordy was unfastening it. Then there was a jerk, a series of them as the boy knotted it in turn about the Salarika.

"Take your time," Rees called softly. "Test the knot, Gordy."

"I will," the promise arose out of the ground

where dust motes still danced upward. "Ready!"
Gordy's pipe was echoed by a pull on the rope.
Rees began to haul it. At least that second cave
in seemed to have taken all the loosened earth
with it. Though the rope still sawed the lip of the
pit, no more of the soil gave way. A small hand
waved suddenly above the surface and the claw
nails of the Salarika dug into the ground as the
child helped to pull herself over and out.

Rees drew her to him, loosened the knot
Gordy had tied, and threw the rope back. The
Salarika crouched against his legs, tonguing the
gash in her arm, shivering throughout her small
body. But Rees had to get the boy out before he
could make a closer examination of her hurt.
When Gordy was back on firm ground once again
Rees knelt beside the little alien, gently drew her
hurt arm across his knee—and then froze as he
saw those pricks in the grayish skin, pricks already marked a brownish tinge.

"Ka thorns!" Rees whispered. One of the most
devilish devices in a Croc hunter's armory. And
one for which there was just one antidote. Rees
bit hard on his lower lip. He had an aid kit in the
roller, but he could inventory its contents too
easily, just as he could also visualize that shelf
back in the lab where stood a slender container
of green fluid, the one outstanding achievement
of Dr. Naper's Ishkurian research; an answer to

the poison of Ka thorns, as well as to several other fatal jungle-fostered deaths. The Salarika in his arms was going to die, almost as painfully and horribly as had the rest of her family back at the post. And there was nothing he could do about it, nothing but think of that container and its contents, which might be as far away as Terra itself now.

Gordy must have heard that whisper. Now he laid his hand on Rees' shoulder, his eyes big and wide. "The medicine, Rees, that's good. You can give her that, make her well. Dad said it always works!"

They had all been so proud at the mission of that discovery. But it was lost now, along with the men who had made it. Just as the child who now lay across his knees was lost. If he only had the container out of the lab!

To return would be the wildest folly. They had only one hope for escape, to head quickly for the eastern mountains and the plantations at their feet. The charge in the roller motor, Rees could not be sure it would last that far. To go back to the mission where even now the Crocs could be crawling . . .

A hand with golden fur across its back raised towards his face. Again sounded that pleading whimper he had heard from the pit. Rees got to his feet, cradling the slight, soft body against his shoulder. He was a fool, a mad fool, but he was going back. The roller was, in its way, a small moving fort, and he knew the territory about the mission as well as if every portion of its expansion was imprinted on his brain.

Back in the machine Rees settled the Salarika on the blankets once again and then started the motor. The stream in which the jungle car rested angled slightly to the right, its course must run in the general direction of the mission. Rees squinted at the position of sun and shadow about him. He had about an hour, he judged, until the onset of twilight. If he could conceal the roller, visit the mission at dusk—

"Where are we going, Rees?" Gordy wanted to know.

"Back for the medicine," the young man replied, his plans crystalizing. Hide out the roller, so leave the children in a measure of safety, he knew where to do that. He would make the rest of the way on foot. His blaster carried a full charge and he would be prepared for an attack. Which the victims of the morning Massacre had not. If the lab had not been looted . . .

The Salarika was moaning pitifully three quarters of an hour later as the Terran stopped the car under the overhang of bushes he had planned as a base. He forced her to drink from the canteen, getting as much of the liquid down her as he could. Then he gave Gordy his orders. No leaving the roller, the sonic curtain kept on, and to stay out of the driver's seat, back on the blankets with the girl. There was a chance that even if the Crocs sighted the jungle car they might think it deserted and leave it alone. Crocs did not like machines, none of the hunters and guides had ever chosen to ride in it when they went hunting with Vickery. And Rees knew that part of the feeling against off-worlders was rooted in the importation of such travel devices.

Rees slipped into the brush, watched Gordy lock on the sonic, and then made his way to the blocks of the mission buildings. He circumvented the 'copter park, sniffing. Croc stink, yes, but already fading. The Terran began to believe that the raiders of the morning had not returned. The beaker would be on the lock shelf under a force shield, in his uncle's lab office. And the force shield, as were the cupboards in the living quarters, were sealed to a palm lock. Luckily Dr. Naper had taken the precaution a month earlier of setting that lock to the pattern of every adult Terran living there, otherwise Rees' errand would have been fruitless.

The lab door was in full sight of the courtyard. Any scout from a Croc band would be able to sight the Terran before he got in from that direction. But there was another entrance, one only desperate measures would force on him. Rees crept behind the living quarters, got down on his hands and knees, running his left hand over the ground while he still grasped his blaster in the right. His fingers found the grip under the sliding gravel and he jerked up the trap door giving on the water tanks. Smells, none of them too pleasant, arose from below, but they were not Croc.

He found the ladder, edged down into moist dark, holstering his weapon so he could feel along the wall with one hand as he clung to his support with the other. A lever to be pulled back, answered by a round opening on the cramped repair tunnel to serve the pump system. Rees scrambled into that, wriggling along on his belly, fighting down the almost panicky fear he always had of tight, dark quarters. If he had not given Permal a hand down here, much against his will, last month, he would not even have known of the existance of this under-the-floor slit which ran the full length of the lab building.

"Two, three . . ." His shoulders scraped from wall to wall, his hair brushed the roof over him. He was counting in a whisper the outlets. "Four!" This was it. He would come out in the lab, then he had only to get around the corner into the office.

The exit seal was stiff. Rees beat against it with his doubled fist, his impatience becoming fear as the outlet stubbornly refused to yield. He could retreat to the third opening. There, it was giving!

Light lanced in at him. No hum of motor, but the wall lights were on. And Croc stink, also other smells, the reek of chemicals, of burnt stuff.

Rees knew that the exit was under one of the stationary sinks which would afford him partial cover as he crawled out. And as soon as he was free of the repair tunnel his blaster was back in his hand.

Though his view of the room was greatly foreshortened, the Terran could see the wreck of the lab. Broken tubes and containers, smears of chemicals, covered the floor.

Avoiding crushed glass, Rees crawled free of the sink, crouched to listen. Three strides would take him to the door of the office. He stood up. Several yards away was a huddle of stained rags. Rees averted his eyes. No use to investigate that closer.

On the office threshold was a wide sear of brown fluid. Croc smell strong enough to chrun Rees' already queasy stomach. One of the raiders had fallen there. In the last few moments of his life Dr. Naper had accounted for one of his murderers, made such an impression on the enemy that the body pinned by darts to the desk inside was headless. The Terran's skull would be as preserved as that of an enemy warrior dead in battle. After one sickened glance Rees kept his attention strictly on what had brought him there. The beaker was still intact, the brilliant emerald of its contents seeming to glow. He inserted his forefinger in the waiting hole below that shelf, twisted right and then left, to brush the sensitive spot within its core with his flesh.

A ghostly shimmer of light as the force field flashed off. Rees caught up the tube and then the record tape box by it. Uncle Milo and the mission might never have any other monument but that discovery, and to take this with him would be his last gesture for the project of which he had been so unwilling a part.

Back down the tunnel, holding the tube in his mouth for safe keeping, the tape box digging into his chest as he inched his way along. Luck seemed to be his and that gave him a prick of doubt, it was too easy. The "hunch," that odd form of awareness which could not be defined but which was inbred in his kind, fostered by his early education, was delivering a warning which became stronger as he emerged from the tunnel into the tank. The blackness in there was complete and again fear bit at him. What if he could not raise the trap door again, was trapped in here? He could always go back through the lab. Yet his sensitive inner alarms told him that something had gone wrong, that he was now in a pinch of danger. He did not know what or why threatened. Go back or on? Try to leave the lab through the courtyard, or raise the door here—perhaps to find himself facing a ring of waiting Crocs.

Rees climbed the ladder, braced himself under the door, put his palm to that barrier and tensed. Then he sent the door hurtling up and out with all the strength he could put into one vigorous shove. It slammed down on the ground, showering sand and gravel. His blaster was out and ready, but he was facing nothing at all save the creeping shadows.

Up and out, a heave and a roll, bringing him free of the tank and under a fringe of bushes where he lay, trying to control his hurried breathing, listening, smelling.

Neither ear nor nose added anything concrete to back that inner warning bell. If the Crocs were on the hunt, they were not yet near enough to betray themselves after the usual manner. Rees got to his knees and then his feet. He put the tube under his shirt with the tape, to give an ever present notice of their presence against his stomach muscles.

Too easy, far too easy. He was thinking that as he went, just before he stumbled, even as he fell forward, that he had been tripped up by a skillfully aimed throw stick. With a writhing which wrenched his back painfully, Rees turned just as he hit the ground, brought his blaster up to fire.

A split second, that was all he had to deflect the beam of his weapon. For the body lunging at him, a short hand axe swinging up, was not the brown scaled monstrosity of a tribesman, but a lithe, furred, silvery creature. He smelled the aroma of Salarika perfume as his attacker half fell on him, the axe coming down.

Pain, and dark, soft slur of words. Rees lay in a torment hardly aware of himself save as a focal point for pain.

"Come, come . . ." Flashes of more pain as his body was shaken. He blinked at a world which tilted about him crazily, and then was able to see those slanted green-blue eyes staring into his, as if by the very intensity of that demanding glare they could arouse him to coherent understanding.

Nails which were closer to claws pricked the skin on his shoulders as the hands of the Salarika supported him in a sitting position. The scent of the alien was familiar. Rees blinked again. No, this was not the cubling he had left curled sick and in pain back in the roller. Golden fur was blue-silver here. And the newcomer was an adult, equaling him in height if not in body structure. For the stranger was also a female, delicately made. However, her grasp was steel strong and she seemed well able to hold up his limp body.

The fine fabric of her upper robe was fringed into rags from her gemmed waist belt down and only three of the encircling wealth of scent bags still dangled from frayed ribbons.

"Zannah, where is Zannah?" Her voice was a low purr which arose from the depths of her throat, her eyes cold slits.

Rees tried to collect his thoughts in spite of the pain in his head.

"Zannah!" the Salarika woman repeated sharply, a hint of hiss in her Basic.

"Little, little girl?" Rees asked groggily.

"Yiss." This hiss was more strident. "Where isss sheee?"

"Roller—back in the roller," the Terran managed to answer.

She was already on her feet, her nostrils expanded, her head turning slowly as she sniffed, until she faced the direction from which he had originally come. Then she took two or three springy steps before she turned, impatience expressed in every line of her body, to look at him. Rees tried to stand, swayed wildly. She darted back to catch him. The Salarika might have given the impression of delicacy, but her strength as she lent it to his support was all he could have asked of a Terran male.

Just how they did make their way back to the roller Rees was never quite sure. His companion retraced the path he had taken, towing him with her, and the Terran was sure she found the way by scent. The first thing he was truly conscious of, was landing on the seat of the machine while his companion crowded over and past him to the children in the storage compartment. He caught at her plush-furred arm.

"Ka thorns'—" Rees had difficulty in finding the right words. "Take some of this, moisten cloth, lay it on the wound, quickly!"

Clawed fingers caught the tube and he leaned forward to rest his head on the arms he had crossed on the control half-wheel. Rees had to rest so for a long moment until the weaving world about him settled into stability and he could fumble at the aid kit. The Terran mouthed the tablets he had sought dry, swallowing convulsively to force them down. Then his headache dulled into a bearable throb, and his vision cleared. A delicate explosion by finger tip told him that over his left ear the scalp was broken, but the blood there was already congealing. Either his own efforts at escape or a belated realization of his identity on the part of the Salarika had saved him from a cleft skull.

"Rees, you are hurt!" Gordy leaned over his shoulder, inspected the damage with wounded, surprised eyes.

"Not too bad. Look in the stores, Gordy, get four Viv-ra-packs and open them."

Rees continued to sit and let the tablets work while the boy brought out the small tins. One Rees left in Gordy's hands, one he put on the seat beside him. The other two he offered to the Salarika woman. The child lay in her arms, a cloth with bright green splashes on it wrapped around the injured arm. Rees indicated the pressure point on the ration pack.

"Press, it heats and then opens," he told her. She nodded.

"Where do you go?" she asked as she put one can to Zannah's lips.

"Without a 'copter our only chance will be one of the big plantations, probably Wrexul's."

"This machine can take us there?"

"I don't know, we can only try. Tell me," he must have an answer to his question, "Why this? You could see I wasn't a Croc." He raised his hand to his head well away from the tender area about the wound.

"I did not see until just before I struck. I scented—Zannah." One of the nails flicked a scent bag at the child's girdle. "I knew that one of the children was gone, might have been taken by the snake-ones. There was their stink about also, very strong."

"So you thought I was a Croc that had taken her? Anyone else escape from the trading post?"

She shook her head. "I am Isiga, second-companion in the house of Lord Sakfor. The snake-beasts, they came to trade as usual, and their stink, it made me sick, for I have only been on Ishkur for two moons. So I went into the far part of the garden until they would go. Then I heard the screams and there was burning between me and the house, they had set fire to the oganna bales waiting there for shipping. So I hid in a tree place. Afterwards . . ." Her ears were skull flat, her fur-hair roughened and party erect. "They hunted but they did not find me. Then I crossed Zannah's trail also and knew that she had run from that evil.

"But with her were other scents, those of you people. So I hoped that she had been found and was at the mission. But when I came here I found again that the snake-beasts had struck. I think by then," her tongue swept across her lips. "I was not clear in my mind. All I could see was the snake-beasts and what they had done and could do again to the little one. So when I caught her scent, if only faintly, and gave the rally cry to which she did not answer, then I believed I was to avenge one already dead—"

"Anyway you didn't carry that through all the way," Rees commented wryly. "It's getting dark.

As soon as I think we can get by without being sighted, I'm going to set this car on hop and head for the mountains. If we continue in luck we ought to be able to raise Wrexul's by dawn."

"That is well," she gave prompt assent to his plan.

Five

As Rees guided the roller toward the eastern heights his thoughts continued to play with the wonder as to why they had not met the Crocs once more. The natives had struck the mission and post with vicious ruthlessness. Then, they had seemingly, vanished into thin air—or the jungle. Croc hunters were expert trackers, tireless on any trail. How had the fugitive off-worlder been able to avoid them so far? Rees' efforts at concealment would have been easy for them to spot. And he did not believe that the natives had been so sated with bloodshed that they would willingly allow the escape of aliens.

Maybe time had something to do with this lull which made him so uneasy. The First Fasts: normally this was the season of native withdrawal to the inner sanctuaries of the High Trees, a district of which the off-worlders had heard but where no non-Ishkurian had ever penetrated. Because this was a period of intense Ishkurian preoccupation with their own affairs had been the very reason the withdrawal of the last Patrol policing force had been scheduled for this date, when most of the natives would be out of contact. Had the massacre on the fringes of stellar civilization been only an isolated gesture before the Crocs began their annual pilgrimage? Rees hoped so, but he could not be sure.

There was a stir beside him. Isiga slid fluidly across the barrier between the driver's seat and the storage space to join the Terran.

"The children sleep," she reported, "Also, it is well with Zannah."

"Why didn't you traders leave when the red alert came from Nagassara?" Rees asked. Mission and trading post had had little contact. But he knew something of the Salariki temperament. Sakfor's stubborn remaining past a warning was a puzzle; the aliens of the trader's species were noted for prudence and wariness.

A small sound came through the dark a hiss of feline anger. "Lord Sakfor was made a promise from the lips of the High Tree Ishgil. Traders were needed, so it was said. There would be nothing for us to fear."

"Apparently that was not true." Rees kept his eyes on the dials before him. In the dark he had to depend much upon the auto-pilot.

"So someone shall learn the result of such split tongue talk!" The cold confidence in that was a threat, or rather another kind of promise. Salariki civilization was based on a feudal organization. Such a tragedy as this which had struck down Sakfor's household would, on the trader's home world, instigate a blood-feud to be taken up by his kinsmen of all degrees. But there would be none to answer such a rallying on Ishkur.

"You think," she was indeed reading his thoughts now, "that one female of a household can not draw a knife and call for the rightful deaths of the enemy. For the moment, no. But the time will come. I am now Name-Head."

She was right! Rees was startled. Under certain conditions, which seldom materialize except in extreme instances such as this, the living adult survivor of a family, whether male or female, became the Name-Head of the victim clan. It was within providence that the woman beside him could demand vengeance from the Truce Court of her own planet and even so set an inter-world war ablaze.

"First," Rees pointed out, "we ourselves, will have to be safely out of this."

"You believe that these Wrexul people will still be at the plantation?"

"If they haven't voluntarily withdrawn, and there was no hint of their doing that the last I heard, they would be in better shape to meet an attack than any other off-world holding this side of the mountains. They fortified their headquarters buildings last season and have a private force of off-world police."

In the reflected light of the instrument panel

he caught a shimmer as she moved and the silvery fur-hair on her arms gleamed.

"And if the Wrexul staff are gone?" she asked.

"Lady," Rees gave her the proper form of address," you had better pray to what God or Spirits of Power you own that they *are* there. We have an energy change in this machine which, with luck, will last to lift us that far. After that, well, there is no way of crossing the mountains in a roller. And I do not think such a journey is possible on foot."

"I thank you that you speak plainly with me," she said after a short pause. "But tell me this also, you have much experience of jungle ways, you are certain we could not travel on foot?"

"Not with the children. I am not even certain a trained Survey Scout could get through, with the Crocs out hunting."

"Our future lies then on the edge of a knife blade, and if the blade cuts . . ." Again that shimmer of silver, she had given a very Terran shrug. "Listen now, Lord Rees . . ." He was startled at that formal title. Though she had just assumed the head-ship of her own clan, she was granting him equality on the terms of her own world, a rare concession for one of the aloof Salariki. "If such a failure is upon us I would wish this, that we go as best we can into the high places, for I have heard that the snake-beasts do not favor the cold and snow in the peaks. Then, should there be no chance of any future for us, we take the warriors' way, going so Behind the Seas, our bodies undefiled. Or do you of Terra not believe that such a course is right and proper?"

"To me that sounds proper," he assented, "if it must be done. We of Terra believe that much; that children and women should not be allowed to fall into the hands of such as the Crocs while men still live."

"Yet there was a woman of your breed at the mission," Isiga pointed out. "And she died so."

"There were divided minds at the mission. Some believed that because they had lived here for many years and treated the Crocs with kindness and fairly, they had nothing to fear."

"Kindness! Fairly!" Her head went up, she made a hissing accusation of each word. "What is kindness, fair treatment, for aliens? To the Salariki kindness is first for his companions-of-the-inner-court and the cublings he fathers there, then to his clansmen. He does not waste good will lightly on strangers without the courtyards. Fairness, yes, that he practices with all, as long as the Peace Flag flies and no man arms for war. Kindness, fairness—to the Salariki those words have one meaning—to Terrans another—to the snake-beasts yet a third. We walk in the patterns set by our ancestors, how can we change to other trails and expect to discover no pitfalls in them? Those who believed the snake-beasts thought the same thoughts, they were fools!"

"Well, they have paid for their folly," Rees said heavily.

"Yet I do not think you were of a like mind. Why did you stay?"

"Because Dr. Naper, the head of the mission, was my chief-of-clan." He put into Salariki idiom the relationship with his uncle. "I was a warrior of the household."

"Then it was fitting that you stayed," she agreed instantly. "Yet you were not one of them in thought, for they were not a people going armed and ready for war."

"You seem to know a great deal about them." Rees was rather puzzled. Dr. Naper and the rest of the mission personnel had certainly not fraternized with the post. And he himself had been so much of the time off in the jungle with Vickery, trying to escape an atmosphere where too often his beliefs gave offense, that he had not had much contact with the post either, having seen Sakfor only twice since the Salariki party arrived six months previously.

A sound which might equal a Terran chuckle came from his seat companion. "In this place if a pat-gru flower blooms a sun before its time there is talk of such a wonder for half a moon. Do you not think that curiosity led us to speculate concerning the only other off-worlders within reach? We knew what food you ate, what beds you rested upon, what clothing you wore, and what thoughts you held or, at least, how you expressed those thoughts in deeds and words. Thus we knew well that those of the mission did not believe in walking a road of warriors. Thus, how easily fighters were able to gobble them up!"

Rees was stung. Isiga only repeated what he thought to be the truth. Terran could criticize Terran but to hear that scorn in an alien voice made him begin a retort he choked off in mid-word.

"But the Salariki al—"

"The Salariki also were victims? You speak that which is right. So we may see that both of our peoples have been fools, each in our own fashion," she replied. "Now we can only prepare not to fail again. Ah!"

A silver finger tip beckoned his attention, pointing to the right. They had taken to the course of the river as soon as the sky had darkened into night, using the faintly phosphorescent water, cascading from a source somewhere in the eastern mountains, for a guide to ground the roller's touching between soaring leaps. The jungle vegetation, discovering no rooting room on the rocky verges of the stream, was a black mass well to either side of the water's path. Here and there sparkled a lamp-bush, eeriely green-blue, drawing to its deadly trap by that light the night flying things it fed upon.

But the color in the night to which Isiga pointed was no lamp-bush. This was a leaping burst of flame, flame consuming some highly combustible fuel, such as the energy blocks necessary to power a roller or 'copter.

Rees hazarded a guess as to the source, one which shook him in spite of the bleak forecasts he had forced earlier on himself. "Ffalow's!"

"The relay station for the Patrol flights over mountain," she added to that identification. "But would there have been any supplies left there to burn? I thought they had closed that down two weeks ago."

"They might have left a cache, as an aid to the mission, or to your post. Uncle Milo didn't say anything about such. But he was so opposed to the idea of withdrawal for the mission that he wouldn't have done so, even if the District Officer had notified him."

"The blocks would have been carefully stored and protected."

"Exactly!" The Terran snapped agreement. "The Crocs are moving east. That fire couldn't have been set more than a few moments ago."

"They go to Wrexul's to raid everything off-world this side of the mountains." It was as if she thought aloud.

"I'd say that's it," Rees agreed. "They know, or think they know, that there won't be any force sent out this way from Nagassara. They probably plan to clean up quickly and then go on their pilgrimages."

This could well explain where the Crocs had gone. Suppose the natives had put only a limited force of jungle fighters into the field? The raiders had begun with the mission, then jumped the post, were now moving purposefully eastward. If so the roller now had to pass a Croc task force, pass through or over natives who were firm in their design to wipe out all off-worlders this side of the mountains.

"So we must pass them." Again Isiga's mind matched his.

"Yes."

Eye of the Spider, see through your enemy's organ of vision. Needful, yes—but possible? Rees shook his head against a surge of fear. He *couldn't* insert himself inside a sloping, armorplated Croc skull, see through a pair of those slit-purpiled eyes. He didn't even know if the murderous forces moving east were jungle aborigines, or those who had had enough contact with off-worlders to have garnered a paper-thin patina of stellar civilization, enough of it to have their mental processes slightly twisted into more recognizable patterns of plan and follow-through.

Rees' knowledge was speedily augmented. Above the roller, but a little ahead, a cleaver of white light cut the night, sliced towards them as might a headsman's knife.

Completely blinded Rees gripped the control wheel fiercely as the roller bucked, rode up to an almost verticle position on the back wave of the force flash. He feared that they would flop over upside down. Then that buck became a sideslip to the left, carrying the machine away from the river towards the jungle. Rees fought to level out, to bring the roller out of that erractic and broken hop to ground safety.

Roller treads bit on a solid surface. Then they bounced into the air again, slammed sidewise against a whip of vegetation which gave under the blow, so the machine slewed into the mat of growth. Behind him Rees heard the screams of the frightened children. Then he realized another pair of hands had joined his on the control wheel, that Isiga was lending her strength to his in an effort to ground them.

Somehow they hit the level once more, or approximate level. Still unable to see more than the fiery flash before his eyes. Rees judged that the nose of the roller was higher than its stern, for their bodies were jammed hard against the back of the seat.

"A force beam!" Isiga's cry made sense. The Terran felt her fur-hair brush against his arm and shoulder as she turned to the children. Then her voice was a soothing purr as she spoke to them.

Rees cupped his hands over his eyes. For a moment of icy panic he was shaken. Was he really blind? Or had the flash only dazzled him temporarily? A force beam! Some one of the Croc mop-up squad had the knowhow to use, and the possession of, a Patrol weapon. Had the Ffalow's station still been manned—and over-whelmed in a native rush, so the off-world weapons had fallen into Croc claws? Force beams were strictly security limited weapons. How *could* the Crocs have them?

"But *how* natives had gotten that piece of armament was certainly no problem of the fugitives; what they did with it was. Rees groped out, caught at a furred arm.

"Listen!" he demanded urgently. "We did come down on the left bank of the river, didn't we?"

"That makes a difference?" she said quickly.

"I'm sure that beam was grounded on the right

"We did move to the left. What is the matter with you?" Her voice rose a note or two.

"Eyes—that flash—I can't see yet."

A sharp hiss of breath. Then her arm moved. Rees felt a faint touch of air against his lips, guessed she was passing her hand back and forth across his face.

"Temporary." He hoped that was true. How had she escaped similar blinding? Perhaps her head had been turned so that she had not looked directly at the flash.

"How are we fixed?" he asked in the next breath.

Isiga moved about in the seat, once leaning across him as if to see what might lie on the far side of the roller. When she spoke her voice was even, giving a concise report.

"We rest on flattened brush. But there is a tree of some size leaning from the front part of the machine so we are not level."

"Behind us?"

"More brush."

"No trees?" Salariki eyesight at night was far better than Terran, as he knew. She must be able to see in greater detail.

"None of any size."

Rees moved one hand in a sweep over the instrument panel. If the roller itself just had suffered no harm from their rough landing . . .

"I am going to try backing," he told her. "But you'll have to watch and guide me."

He fumbled for the right button, pressed it down. The roller lurched from side to side, shook in a way which told him that much of the surface of both treads must be supported on broken bushes above the ground level. Now the machine rocked back and forth, but it was also creeping in retreat, the tree support in front holding them less high. There was a crackling of brush all around. How long did they have before the Crocs swam the river to bag their victims?

And how badly was the roller damaged by the backwash of the beam? Rees clung to one small hope—that the attackers might have seen that erratic crash landing and that it appeared, from a distance, worse than it really was. The natives might now believe they were firmly grounded. If that were true the Crocs would take their own time about following them, sure of their own ability to track down and take any survivors.

The jungle car rested on an even beam now, its treads getting a grip on something solid through a mush of leaves, twigs and splintered branches. Also the brilliant pinwheels before Rees' eyes were fading.

"Now," the Terran appealed again to his companion, "any clear sky around except straight up?" The roller was no 'copter, it could not be jumped from a stand into a vertical rise.

"Not here."

To go out of the jungle to the open of the river bank was to offer themselves as an easy sitting target for the beam operator. They could plow ahead, waiting to find a clearing big enough to afford them the necessary hop run.

"Where's the most open ground path?"

Again he felt her move on the seat, guessed she was making a careful survey of their surroundings.

"Trees ahead and to the right. Only brush to the left but that way will return us to the river bank."

"Behind?" The roller was responding sluggishly.

"Yes, it is better that way."

They began a painful retreat, the machine swiped and beaten by branches and vines. Rees became aware that the sonic curtains had failed and a pounding on its button aroused no answering hum. Insect life—Rees flinched as a pin-point of fire lanced the side of his neck just above the shoulder meeting. But this was no time to worry about such minor matters.

"Wait!" Isiga's hand clamped down on his forearm, until her nails cut his skin. "A little, just a little more and you can turn. No trees there, just bushes and many vines."

No trees maybe, but vines could be worse in

their way. However, he could only try. Rees waited for her cry of "Now!" and swung the control wheel. The roller obeyed awkwardly and they crackled on, beating a path through the resisting jungle wall.

Six

"Get your head down, keep the children back there, well under cover!" Rees ordered and crouched lower on the seat. The whipping lashes of brush and broken vine swept across the top of the roller as they crunched a path onward. The young man blinked frantically. Shadows against shadows, a faint difference in the quality of light, the pin-wheels fading. He gave a sigh of relief; the blindness was only temporary as he had hoped.

"The dials, to the left, second on the panel on your side," he got out breathlessly, his words shaken from his lips by the jolts of the roller. "Any change of the indicator?"

"The bar points straight up."

"Bang on it with your hand!" Rees rapped out, afraid to accept that without a test.

"Now the bar swings," she reported a moment later, "but it returns to the same position."

"Then it's still working—and we aren't followed yet."

But why not, Rees thought. Unless, unless their over-the-river crack-up had looked much worse than it was to any Crocs watching. The enemy might deem them grounded; either dead or else easy meat for more leisurely follow-up, to be picked up later after they had wiped out the last off-world pockets in this section. He said as much to Isiga.

"Since I, too, thought we were finished," she observed, "perhaps they are not to be blamed in judging our descent fatal. How long now to Wrexul's?"

"I don't know. If we could appeal for a com cast we could ride a finder beam in. As it is we'll have to depend on the spy-scout, and make sure it doesn't guide us to a Croc raiding party. But Crocs with a force beam! They can break . . ." He stopped short, aware at last of what that fact could mean.

"A force beam," Isiga finished for him a greater calm then he believed he could summon at the moment, "could also burn a path through the Wrexul defenses, is that not so?"

"Yes. But if our people knew that the Crocs were so armed, they could do something."

"What?" she asked bleakly.

What indeed? A well defended post such as Nagassara port itself, that could stand up to a force beam, put up a counter-force cast which would send the power of the attacking beam back, to burn out the caster and those who sighted it. But not even Wrexul's would possess protection of that type here. The defenders would not be expecting to front one of the top Patrol weapons in the hands of jungle fighters. Also, primitive jungle hunters would not know how to use it, certainly not with the accuracy which had downed the roller. Someone in that band had had training in modern off-world weapons.

"Wrexul's is our only chance," Rees said dully. "We can't lift over the mountains in this machine." He was beginning to doubt if they were going to roll any distance further here either. The roller was handling in a way which could not be explained by the rough terrain through which they were boring a path. The sonic was out. What about its other protective measures?

"Wait!" Isiga's voice was sharp. "That dial, the bar on it moves now!"

Rees gripped the half-wheel tighter. "In what direction, to what degree?" To him the faint glimmer of the instrument panel was too blurred to read.

"It swings right . . . ten points . . . now more . . ."

"That means the Crocs are across the river. What's ahead of us?"

Her hand was on his shoulder to steady herself

as she stood up in the rocking machine, using her better-than-Terran night sight on the path before them.

"Ahh! Pull up—quick!"

Rees obeyed, and the roller lurched as he applied the cut-off, slewed around in the crushed brush. The flamer! If he could use the flamer! He fully expected to front a Croc attack out of the dark.

"We are near to the edge of a drop," Isiga reported. "How deep a one I do not know, but it is wide. Can we hop it?"

Rees' fingers went to that other button, thrust hard. The machine spurted, but there was no answering surge strong enough to raise it from the mass of vegetation where it rested. He was right, more than the sonic had suffered back there in the crash.

"The hop power is out," he said. What to do now? Try to swing around so he could rake the brush with the flamer? All he had been trying to remember this nightmare day and night about the spider's eye was at last beginning to pay off. He'd be taking the biggest gamble of his life, a bigger one perhaps than he should have. But it could be their only chance.

"Get this," he spoke incisively having made his decision. "I'm going to turn, with my back to the drop. You empty the storage compartments,

fill the canteens from the tank, take all rations—
you can pack it all into those blankets—get the
children ready. As soon as we stop, take them and
the supply packs out of here. Head to the right,
along the edge of the drop. Wait . . ." he un-
fastened the blaster belt with its comfortably
filled holster. "Do you know how to use one of
these? Three pressures of the firing button gives
you maximum, and you'll need that to burn
through Croc belly armor."

"And you?" She took the weapon from him.

"I'm going out in a blaze of fire power as far as
the Crocs are concerned. It's the pattern they
follow when they are cornered in battle. They'll
come up, get the flamer in the face. And then the
roller will buck back into the drop and blow up.
If any of them survive that toasting, they'll think
we all went up with the machine. I'll join you as
soon as I can."

"This machine is too disabled to aid us farther?" Her cool acceptance of their danger was a
steadying support.

"Yes. It might conk out completely at any moment. Now get moving!"

He helped her gather the canteens, the packs
of rations, the aid kit, two bush knives. Then he
handed Zannah out into her waiting arms, saw
Gordy stumble after, the small boy manfully lugging the second blanket bundle. They were gone

and Rees was alone, grimly hoping his choice was the right one. With any luck he should be able to make their pursuers believe that they were all trapped in the disabled roller.

Gingerly he maneuvered the jungle car about, and his suspicions concerning the future were amply proven by the stiff, limited responses to its controls. Once the motor cut out entirely and Rees thought it was gone, until it answered haltingly to his frantic coaxing. He was turned around now, his back to the gulf masked in the darkness, the flamer facing the way the Crocs must come. Luckily his eyes had recovered to the point where he could read the spy-scout dial. Its pointer had swung well past the half-way mark. The Crocs were coming, fast now.

They couldn't carry a beamer, not over this broken ground, unless they had it mounted on a lift platform. And if they also had one of those . . . Rees smiled, a stretch of thin lips which did not in the least denote humor. That would have to come straight along the swath the roller had cleared. The flamer would take it, the beam it transported, and any firing crew riding it, dead center.

The Terran made two other preparations and sat quietly to wait. He regretted the loss of the sonic. The undergrowth flattened in the passage of the jungle car must have been the valued home of countless insects. All Rees could do was trust in the strength of the repellent he had smeared on his skin moments earlier, but that did not guard him against all stings, bites, and the crawling exploration of creeping things he could not see (and did not want to anyway). Waiting; that bit, too, worse than any insect. He began to count mentally, try thus to estimate how far Isiga and the children could have traveled since they left the roller.

Rees' eyes adjusted, and not a moment too soon! Not even Crocs, jungle wise as they were, could mask that object hanging well above the road of the roller, appearing as a blotch against the sky. It swung on and the diffused radiance of a half crushed lamp-bush gave Rees an idea of its outline. So they *were* bringing in the beam on a lift!

The Terran pushed the flamer button. A tongue of raw red fire licked out. It must have caught the lift platform and its burden square on. But Rees did not wait to make sure. His arm shielding his eyes from the glare, he spun out of the seat, clung to the door with one hand, just long enough to kick at the starter. Then he hit the ground and squirmed to his knees, scuttled over a rocky surface which bruised the skin of his plams.

Roller treads grated on the rock as the car groveled backwards. Fires were blazing around as the flamer slewed back and forth, tonguing out in a fan-shaped sweep before the retreating machine. Then that spear of fire pointed skywards as the car teetered on the brink of the drop. Rees, yards away now, dared pause to glance back.

Down it went, toppling back into the gulf. And some of the enemy had survived. The rasping, coughing screeches of the Crocs made a harsh clamor. The Terran took to his heels, hoping that they would congregate on the edge, even start down towards the wreckage. He had hit them hard and they would be swept out of prudence, wanting to take his head. The skull of a valiant enemy was a far better trophy for the High Tree of a clan than that of a victim cut down in a massacre.

Rees gasped as a pain caught him under the ribs. Now he must depend not only on his own speed and agility, but on Isiga's night sight. If the Salarika kept to the edge of the gully as he had ordered, he should catch up with the fugitives before too long. But as he scuttled faster to put as much distance between him and the crash as he could, Rees still waited for the finale he had planned.

That came with more force than he had deemed possible. A crackle of light fiercer than the native sun lit up the Ishkurian landscape, even though its source was at the bottom of the drop. Rees stumbled on, a sound rising from his lips, not quite a laugh. Any headhunters caught in that explosion of a heated motor fed a full stream of energy would no longer be interested in skulls—not even their own!

The leaders of that Croc party must have been operating the force beam on the lift. And Rees could probably count on their having been killed by the flamer. Now if there had been any survivors of the roller explosion they would not be out to track off-worlders. Rees had copied the pattern of their own people when facing overwhelming odds; get the enemy and end one's own life into the bargain.

Only, now he was beginning to worry about Isiga and the children. Surely they could not have gone any farther than this. He slackened pace, trying to see more than the splotches of lamp-bush. Then another light brought Rees to an abrupt stop.

Well overhead, but coasting down on a flight track which would connect with the ground just ahead of him, was a red line, or rather a pin-pricked outline of a monstrous head, jaws agape and every fang a small pulsating coal.

In the roller or even in the open with a blaster, Rees would have been able to face that menace with the confidence of the superior armed. But his knife was no protection against an air dragon in the thing's own territory. This was a creature of the Ishkurian night, using its light celled head to dazzle and terrify its prey into helplessness. And it was on the hunt now but Rees realized he was not the quarry.

The others! All the jungle had come into terrified wakefulness at the noise of the battle. Screams of disturbed flying things, of the small dwellers in the mass of vegetation were a loud uproar, through which the Terran could not hear the ominous flap of those wide skin-and-rib-boned wings. He could only watch that wicked, red-outlined head as the thing approached in a purposeful glide.

Isiga had the blaster, and he knew her sight was excellent. But if she used that weapon to finish off her attacker, she would also advertise to any Croc that the fugitives were still alive. Their sacrifice of the roller would mean nothing and they would be easy prey for trackers.

Rees' feet continued to carry him forward, though he had no glimmering of idea as to what he was going to do with two bare hands against those red coals of teeth and the tearing foretalons which hung below the too-well-defined head.

The air dragon was at tree-top level now, the smaller trees which rimmed the gully, not the towering giants of the true jungle. Those jaws snapped with cruel visibility. The hunter must have caught some flying creature bewildered into flight. But the morsel was too small to satisfy it. Now it hovered, perhaps some ten feet above the ground, the red outline of its head jerking back and forth. Rees gave a gasp of relief, his left hand pressing his aching ribs. What the air dragon sought was under cover.

Unfortunately these things did have some intelligence, that and a habit of stubbornly settling upon one prey and that alone in a night's hunting. The air dragon would continue to patrol above, waiting for its intended meal to break from the protecting cover. And its very presence there, especially in a jungle already awakened and alert, would be a signal to summon others, the ground beasts, those that feasted on the remains after the flier had sated his more fastidious appetite and was gone.

The skull-rats, the progies; those would gather. And a pack of either would flush the dragon's game into the open. Rees had heard Vickery's stories of such combined hunts and knew that the animal collector did not exaggerate in the least. To stay was death of one kind; to move was death of another.

He estimated the circling course of the dragon. It flapped back and forth leisurely, not in the least concerned over the eventual outcome of the action. Rees was as certain as if he could see them clearly that the prey it sought was Isiga and the children. They must be—Rees studied the swing of the red tipped head above—under some bush or thick branched tree, a little to the left and even nearer to the edge of the drop. Perhaps the Salarika had been trying to reach that when the dragon had swooped too near for her to longer expose them to its pounce.

Rees took to cover. Belly flat he wormed a way towards the spot he had fixed upon as the core of the dragon's interest. He must move quickly, before the skull-rats or the progies came!

Then he was flattened under a thin curtain of cover, aware that that red pitted outline of a head swung about, was not pointing towards him! If he were only close enough! There was one action they could combine upon. Or if Isiga could use the blaster with an expert's ease and a narrow beam. With Vickery he would have tried such a move at once but now he must be sure.

Something thudded out into the patch of open cut so invitingly and meancingly on the very lip of the gully. It winked with the reflection of pale light on metal as a spark in the bush from which it had been flung fastened on it in an off and on beam no stronger than the body light of some night insect. The blaster! Isiga must have seen his arrival and was now signalling to him the position of the weapon.

Rees swept out his hands to either side of his body, raking in the muck of old leaves and twigs, hunting for a fallen branch he might use to reach the blaster. There was nothing to be found save some wood so rotted it crumbled to evil-smelling powder in his grasp.

The blaster was there in the open, the air dragon alert and ready overhead. Its circle was tight above the clearing. The longer Rees waited the less he would be able to nerve himself to what he had to do now. The Terran set his teeth, tensed his body.

He did not really leap, rather he threw himself low, as he might have done in tackling a runner, concentrating on that weapon. As his hand fell upon it, he flopped over on his back, swinging the blaster up so that it pointed skyward from his chest. And he stared wildly up into pure nightmare.

The monstrous head was not just a red outline now. All its horror bloomed in the sudden beam of a handlight. And that ray dazzled it for just the second Rees must have to thumb the blaster to narrow beam and fire. He saw the pencil of energy leap at the gaping mouth and then kicked into a roll which carried him on toward the bush from which the hand light had come.

A clawed foot raked, scraping along the Terran's side, tearing clothing from his body. But the strength of that stroke flung him on and away. Rees heard a scream of terrifying volume as he came up hard against fur and flesh and lay gasping for air.

Somehow he squirmed up into a sitting position, the blaster again ready. But there was nothing out there to aim at, neither in the air or on the ground.

"What?" he began.

"It went over and down." Fingers fastened on his shoulder. "You are hurt?"

Went over where? Rees tried to make sense of that as the hands swept down his arm to his scraped side, touched some scratch there to stinging life. Into the gully! That's what she meant; the air dragon must have been so severely wounded it had fallen into the gully!

"You shot a dragon!" Gordy's voice was a breathy cry of triumph. "It's head went all smash! That's just what it did!"

"And you have taken no great harm." Her hands were busy applying some substance to his side in swift, competent strokes.

"We've got to get out of here," Rees assembled his wits to the point where common sense was again in command. He still did not quite believe that this had really happened, that he had pulled off their second wild gamble of the night.

"Down the gully," Isiga told him, "there is a sheltered way. I had just found it when the dragon came. And there are signs of a path, we can not be too far from the plantation."

"Then let's get going!" Rees urged.

Seven

"No signs of life." Rees lay flat, his chin supported on an arm stretched across before him. A screen of scarlet-tipped grass stood between him and the sharply sloping drop toward a barrier which caught and reflected the greenish sunlight. He could not be wrong; the sentry towers at the four corners of that enclosure, the size and substantial structures the wall protected, said this was Wrexul's. But nothing moved from one of those buildings to the next, the place had a deserted look.

"The 'copter park," Isiga was beside him, her silver fur-hair and grey skin blending better than the Terran's torn clothing and pink-tan hide with the color of Ishkurian soil and grass roots, "there is nothing there."

Rees had already noted that disappointing fact. The off-world staff could have sealed their headquarters, taken off in the 'copters, trusting to luck that the trouble would be settled and they could return. From what Rees could sight every building was closed, the gates shut. And he imagined that persona-locks were on. A barrier tuned to Terran body heat would permit his entrance and

Gordy's—but he was dubious about the Salariki. He said as much to his companion.

"We should go there, even if your people have left?"

"They didn't take the com with them. And that must be on direct beam with the port. If I could make contact with the authorities a 'copter could be sent be on robo-control."

She nodded. "But what if the snake-beasts behind us have another force beam?"

Yes, what if their brush back by the gully in the night had not knocked out the full enemy force? The rest of the Ishkurians could be ringed around down there, just waiting for a chance to get into the plantation stronghold. There was a wide swath cleared of all vegetation, fire burnt to the soil, about the four sides of the barrier. That had clearly been done since the last full rain, the black ash was still to be noticed. Someone had ordered that destruction as a reasonable precaution against any creep attack. In order to get to the gates Rees must cross that open. And only the gates, one of those two, would pass him as soon as his body heat activated their controls. Then, once in, he must locate the control room, clear the persona-locks for Isiga and Zannah. Or else head directly for the com, send his message and return here to await the arrival of a rescue 'copter. Rees outlined the alternative plans to the Salarika.

"You believe that this 'lock' is set against us, that neither I nor Zannah could pass it?"

"Wrexul's had a straight Terran staff. Your people seldom sign wage contracts with Terran firms."

"That is true. Is it now a matter of time?"

"Not too closely, I hope. And down there, with that barrier in working order, the Crocs couldn't get at us. Not unless they do have another force beam."

"So many guesses, and so easy to make the wrong one," Isiga commented. "But for this I am willing to throw the quass sticks and take what count of red Fortune offers. To be within walls which hold off snake-beasts, that would make one's heart beat less fast, smooth one's hair sleek again."

"Then stay right here, all of you," Rees cautioned. "When you see me return to the gate, then make a run for it. I will cover you with the blaster."

He shouldered the larger pack of their supplies and began to run. Under his boots the slope seemed to stretch itself, making a longer dash through the open than he had estimated when under cover above. Rees skidded against the surface of the barrier, his shoulder meeting it with force enough to jar painfully along his tender side.

Was the gate on persona-lock? The Terran waited breathlessly, clinging to that hope. Certainly the staff would not have set the combination to any but a general Terran body heat. There was too much chance that any one individual might not return. But at least Rees had not been burnt to a crisp at contact, or given a brain washing sonic blast. And he was sure the Wrexul people must have left some warm and fierce welcome for any Crocs daring to nose around.

There was a click, hardly louder than the sounds made by some grass insects. A portion of the wider gateway to his left slid back. One-man heat, one-man door, that figured. Rees leaped through and the panel went back into place behind him.

The control room, which should hold the com also—which—where? Rees surveyed the buildings and tried to guess their uses. Finally he chose one which was attached by a short corridor to the living quarters. Its outer door must also have been set on persona-lock because when he was still a foot or so away it folded into the frame.

This was a power room right enough. And one showing signs of hurried abandonment. A cup stained with dregs of Terran coffee sat on a shelf beside an instrument panel, a scarf trailed from the back of a built-in seat. Rees made a hurried examination of the board beside the coffee cup.

While the mission had never used a persona-lock, in fact Uncle Milo had dismantled part of it three months ago to take out the pack motor for the repair of a lift beam, Rees knew what he was searching for. And that dial with its attendant row of buttons was easy to find.

One second to press full release, then he was running back to the outer gate. He waved his hand high over his head.

Gordy came down the slope first, carrying the other bundle. The boy stumbled once, went to a scratched knee, and when he got up, smeared the back of his hand across his dirty face. Isiga, carrying Zannah, padded light-footedly up behind the child, the encouraging words she used to spur him on reaching Rees merely as a sing-song purr. The Terran sprinted out as they neared, swept up Gordy, in spite of the boy's indignation, and somehow hustled them all inside the barrier. It was necessary now to close the gate by hand. He slammed it and ran to re-set the lock.

"Food," Isiga pattered along after him. "That's what we need. And have you found the com?"

"Not yet. I'll look for it now." But as Rees went slowly about the room his steps dragged. He staggered once, steadied himself with a hand against the wall. That last spurt through the gate lugging Gordy—it was as if that effort had used up all the reserve of strength on which he had been drawing so heavily since they had left the mission. How long had it been since he had dared to relax, to rest? More than one Ishkurian day. And even now he dared not think of sleep.

"You sick, Rees?" Gordy blinked at him owlishly.

"Just a little tired. Don't you want to go with the Lady Isiga and find something to eat?"

"Where's Mom, Rees, and Dad? You said they'd be here with the 'copter. And I haven't seen them. There's no one here but us. I want my Mom."

For a moment Rees was unable to understand that; his fatigue was like a mental fog. Then he recalled dimly the excuse he had used to cover the tragedy for Gordy yesterday morning.

"They must have gone on again, Gordy." He knew he was fumbling, not handling this well. But he was too tired to be very imaginative. "We'll call a 'copter and go on to Nagassara."

"I don't believe you!" The boy stated, frankly hostile. "I want my Mom and I want her now!"

Rees lurched over to sit down in the chair from which the scarf trailed. The whisp of soft material fluttered to the ground and Gordy pounced upon it.

"This isn't Mom's," he told Rees accusingly. "She hasn't never been here. I'm going home right now, I'm going home!"

"You can't!" Rees' control was on the ragged edge of breaking. He could not deal with a frightened, stubborn child on top of everything else, not now. "Isiga!" He shouted, knowing that he did not have either the will power or the energy to leave the seat and hunt out the Salarika in person.

"You can't make me stay here." Gordy backed toward the door, his face a sullen scowl as he wrung the soft scarf between his scratched and dirty hands. "You can lock me up, but I won't stay! I'm going back to Mom and Dad. Dad's going to get you, Rees Naper, for bringing me away. He said I wasn't to go around with you. You're a bad man, you fight."

"So I fight," Rees repeated grimly. "Well, it's a good thing I know how, whether I like it or not. Listen here, Gordy, you're just tired and hungry and I know you want your mother. But we must get to Nagassara. The Crocs. . . ."

"Dad said 'Crocs' is a bad word!" Gordy's voice was shrill. "You say bad words and you tell lies and I'm not going to stay here!"

He whirled and dashed out of the doorway. Rees got to his feet and stumbled after. The persona-locks—Gordy could pass by them—leave either gate without interference. Rees must reach the child, keep him from leaving the plantation fort.

"You, you let me alone! I'm going home right now!" Gordy struggled in Isiga's grip, hitting and kicking, his voice now a scream of pure hysteria. But, as Rees had discovered earlier, the Salarika's hold was strong. And she not only continued to restrain the boy but bent over him with a soothing croon.

Her eyes met Rees' and he read reassurance in them. This was now woman's business and the Terran trusted the Salarika to handle the rebel. He must go back and hunt for the com.

He had located the unit and was seated before the call mike when she slipped in to join him.

"Gordy?"

He has eaten, now he sleeps. Also I have put a catch on the door. But his purpose is firm. We shall have to watch him. He does not know that those of his inner court are dead?"

"No, how can you tell a child a thing like that?" Rees appealed. "I had to keep him in the roller, away from the mission. So I told him his mother and father had gone, that we would catch up with them later."

"Such evasions always lead to complications," she pointed out. "But, yes, I can understand how you found it too hard to speak the truth to a little one. Perhaps, when he wakes and is quieter, I may be able to tell him something. He is now too angry and frightened to listen."

"I suppose so. The sooner we can raise Nagassara the better!"

"There are those there who are his kin?"

"No." For the first time Rees considered Gordy's future. "No, there's no one and I don't think he even has any close kin off-world. He'll be the responsibility of the mission foundation."

"And you, you have other kin?"

"No. My father was a Survey Scout. He did not return from Rim run. Dr. Naper was my uncle."

Her green-blue eyes regarded his thoughtfully. "We heard that you sought animals in the jungle with the tamer of beasts. You did not work at the mission?"

"Hardly!" His old bitterness was sour and heavy. "Uncle Milo took me away from the Survey Academy, he was strongly opposed to the Service. But he could not make his ideas mine. So now I am neither one thing, nor another!"

"And what will you do when we reach Nagassara?"

Rees shrugged. "I don't know. Join the militia maybe. Hunt up Captain Vickery anyway. We have to get there first."

She flexed her slender fingers, casing and uncasing her claw nails, and there was a spark centering each slit pupiled eyes.

"Yes, that is true, we must reach Nagassara before we can earn a future. But, Lord Rees, keep this in your mind; I am now Name-Head of a clan, a trade clan. In Nagassara you may have more than one chance. Are not Free Traders explorers too?"

Rees blinked, not really taking in the meaning of her words. Nagassara was the width of a mountain range and more away. What did any future beyond the immediate one of trying to reach there mean now?

He pressed the key of the com. The call light sparked on the board. Wrexul's personal call symbols he did not know, so he restoted to those of the mission. And such coming in on the Wrexul beam length would alert any operator at the port to the fact that this was a distress call.

Tip-tap-tock. Rees beat out the pattern. But the plate to receiver remained obstantly blank. The com was alive, sending. Why no answer? Cold squeezed Rees' middle, added to the leaden weight fatigue had hung on his arms and shoulders. Was—was Nagassara already abandoned, had the last spacer lifted? Or had the Crocs erupted all over the planet and crushed the stronghold of the off-world government?

"No answer!" Isiga's fingers hooked, claws fully out, as if she would tear the symbols out of the plate by force. He could hear her heavy breathing through the beat of the key.

"Could—could they have gone? She put one of

his fears into words as desperate moments length-
ened into minutes—two—four—six . . .

"I don't see how." Rees bore down the sending
key. "There may be a mountain storm, those cut
the beams at times. It must be that, it has to!"

He stared at the blank mirror face of the receiver as if by the demands of will alone he could
bring a responsive flash to it. *Tip—tap—tock.*

"Identify!" Imperious, demanding, that single
signal on the key. Two Terrans, he gave their
names and place of origin; two Salariki, cut off
without transportation at Wrexul's, an appeal for
a robo-copter. He reeled that off, began to repeat
the message with the same ragged speed.

"Naper—give name of X-Tee instructor, Survey
Academy five years ago."

Rees stared blankly at the symbols on the mirror, wondering for a dread filled second or two if
he had cracked under the strain, as the message
had no earthly, or galactic, connection with the
S.O.S. he had broadcasted. But the symbols remained there without alteration when he asked
for the reason.

"This is no time to play games!" The Terran
burst out, banging his fist on the edge of the
panel.

"Not games, I think," Isiga said. "There is some
need for them to be sure that you are who you say
you are. Can it be that the snake-beasts are us-

ing coms to call out either would-be rescuers or to gain transportation into Nagassara?"

Rees relaxed. That made some sense. But Crocs using the com units that way? Only they had been armed with a force beam, too, he had to remember that. They were not just up against primitive jungle runners after all.

"X-Tee instructor—Zorkal." Luckily they had asked him to name Zorkal and not, say, the astro-math man. But Zorkal had given Rees extra instruction when he had discovered how keen the young Terran was on X-Tee.

"Set your field guide beam on C-2-59 over Y," the mirror told him, apparently satisfied now that he was Rees Naper in the flesh. "You will have to wait. There is a flash storm in Nass Pass and we can not send the Robo until that clears."

"A storm!" Isiga's voice was close to a sigh. And Rees could have echoed that sound of frustration in a far more vigorous outburst if his weariness was not so complete.

The Nass Pass could be storm blocked for minutes, hours or days. And it was very true that a robo could not fight the winds there and get through with only a ride-beam to bring it in. Rees set the guide as directed and then let his hands fall into his lap. He was literally too worn out to move. Then Isiga's warm clasp on his bowed shoulders roused him a little.

"Come eat, sleep," she purred close to his ear. "You will have time if there is a storm."

"You need rest also," Rees suggested. But he was standing up under her surprisingly strong pull, staggering to the door where she steered him.

She had found supplies left by the plantation staff, produced a meal Rees ate his way through, hardly aware of what he chewed and swallowed, or why, while she sat opposite him at the table drinking some liquid of her own choosing in delicate sips from a cup she held in both hands.

He was in the jungle clearing of Vickery's camp, facing the three walls of cages. And in each cage crouched a Croc, their snouts high, their teeth bared. The horrible stink of their hatred and anger choked him. Now the cage controls were weakening. Rees knew that without actually seeing the give of the latches. And there were no weapons at his belt, nothing but his two bare hands with which to face their charge.

To escape—to escape he must get into one of those plated bodies, see through those red eyes. But how? How did one become a Croc? Yet he must, he must!

Rees was sitting up, gasping, his heart pounding heavily within the wall of his chest. He flailed out with an arm, grazed a body which dodged that blow. Then his gaze steadied on Isiga. He must have been dreaming!

"The robo—it's here!" He got up from the bunk, ready to go.

Rees wavered. Her tone, eyes—the expression in them brought him into full wakefulness. He drew a deep breath and the air seemed to catch in his throat. That smell, that couldn't be any hazy hold over from his dream! Less heavy than the stench of his nightmare, but unmistakable for what it was. Rees whirled to face the window open above the bunk. The breeze pushed in through the sonic unchecked. It was the cool wind of early evening and the gray shadows of dusk fogged out there.

"They've come," he said in a half whisper.

Croc stink; he would never forget it as long as he was able to breathe.

"Have they shown themselves yet?" Rees' head swung back to Isiga.

"No. But that is plain that they are there." She waved a hand at the window and the wind.

"And there must be a lot of them."

"Gordy is gone."

Rees didn't take that in at once. He had been too busy listening, thinking about the force which must now ring in around the plantation fort.

"Gordy . . ." The Terran repeated absently and

118

then the meaning of her report sank in. "How long?" he snapped.

"Zannah says only a half hour perhaps. We searched the rooms first."

Rees ran, heading for the gate, that gate through which only a Terran could pass, which should have meant their safety and escape. But which to Gordy could mean . . . No, not that— please, not that!

Eight

"Gordy!" Rees yelled with the full force of his lungs. There was a faint echo resounding from the higher land, but no other answer. And the gate was closed.

Rees pulled up. "He could be hiding," he said to Isiga who had run along behind him. She shook her silvery head.

"We searched as I told you. Zannah also says he went to look for his mother."

The boy could be anywhere in that wall of vegetation beyond the burned strip. And with the Croc smell this strong. To try to track a missing child in the jungle which was the enemies' own hunting ground was the rankest folly.

Eye of the Spider! Rees froze. He knew, now he knew what was going to happen as clearly as if his brain did occupy one of those armored, saurian skulls, look through the red alien eyes. Gordy was a key, a key to be used to open Wrexul's.

Perhaps the Crocs had already tried to cross the barrier, found the persona-locks past their breaking. Some scout, left on sentry at one of the high points cupping in the stronghold, could have witnessed the fugitives' entrance, marked the ease with which the Terrans had passed the gate. The Ishkurians might have been just waiting for some such chance, and Gordy had given it to them!

Rees turned, began to walk back to the building at a slower pace.

"What is it?" Isiga matched her steps to his. "What is it that you have thought of?"

"Gordy, they won't harm him yet. Because he's their key to the gate!"

"The lock!" Again her voice was a hiss of anger. "They will use him to open the gate for them."

"So they must bring him back to us," Rees held to that fact which was the only one holding a fraction of hope.

"And what do we do?" she wanted to know.

"You and Zannah must wait at the 'copter park, ready if and when it comes. Maybe we can find weapons."

"No, for those I have already looked. There are none left."

"Maybe no apparent ones but I want to see what is in those store rooms." Rees headed purposefully for the windowless building he had marked down as the warehouse.

"That is time locked, I think. I could not open it."

"A lock can be shorted," he snapped.

The dusk was deepening. Night came fast here in the foothills and the darkness would provide cover for the Crocs using Gordy. Lights, they needed floods to cover the whole inner area. Wrexul possessed a flood system, the standards and lamps were in sight.

Rees set about preparing for the attack he knew was on the way. Even if the robo arrived now, they could not leave. Or he could send Isiga and Zannah. But he would have to remain until the natives moved in with Gordy. The robo could be sent back again.

The control room gave him the power of turning on the floods and Rees made a glittering day within the perimeter of the stronghold. He tried to keep his mind on what he must do, tried to forget what could happen to Gordy. But the tightness in him was a physical pain by now.

Now the store rooms! Rees, carrying tools, went to work, making the necessary adjustments to wiring, watched the portal open. Bales, boxes that were the last crop ready to be shipped, supplies from off-world. He tore open boxes, read labels with feverish haste. In the end he brought out his selected loot, rolling two bales into the open before he tore at the sacking bagging their contents.

"Oganna!" Isiga came to him. "What is it that you would do?"

"This." Rees pulled the closely packed leaves apart, the oily drops gathered on their surfaces, pasting them together so that separating them was a task. "Spread these around to wall in the 'copter park. Pile them thick."

"Yes," her eyes held the feral park spark of a hunting cat's. "Yes!" She snatched up an armload of the stuff and sped away. Zannah pattered out of the shadows, her injured arm in a sling. But in the other hand, she, too, picked up a bundle of the oganna and hurried after Isiga.

The flood lights which made day about the barrier were dimmed here by building shadows. Rees did not believe any Croc watchers could be sure what the activity of the off-worlders meant. Croc eyes did not adjust well to bright light. The enemy must now be considering days and means of putting out the floods.

He went on with his leaves, piling them up, watching Isiga and Zannah working to outline the square on their side. Only directly facing the space before the outer gate did Rees leave a break in that low wall of odorous vegetable material.

"That is the last." Isiga came to him, brushing one hand vainly against the other in a useless try to rub away the sticky oil. She saw the gap and glanced from it to Rees with sudden understanding.

"Do you dare?"

"It is that I must," he told her bleakly.

Her fingers arose to her lips and then she jerked

her hand away before they touched her mouth. But those wide feline eyes narrowed.

"Come!" She beckoned him back to the living quarters. There she caught up one of the spider silk blankets. To tear one of those was, Rees had thought, close to impossible. But somehow the Salarika achieved that task, using a knife and her claw nails. She coiled the strips across the table and brought out a basin. Water splashed from the wall tap into that container. Then she knelt before the aid kit, chose tubes and boxes whose contents she had sniffed. Powder and liquid went into the waiting water and was mixed thoroughly by sloshing the bowl back and forth. That done she turned to Rees.

"Your clothing," she indicated the remains of his shirt, the scuffed boot-breeches, "off. I do not know how well this will protect you but it will be better than nothing at all."

He stripped quickly as she soaked the parts of blankets in the basin. Then she went to work deftly to wind the sopping material about him from foot to neck, leaving the binding of his head, with only a narrow opening for eyes, nose and mouth, to the last. The liquid had turned a bright purple-blue and Rees guessed that he must now present a weird appearance, perhaps startling enough to actually work in his favor as a momentary surprise for the Crocs when he had to face them at the breakthrough. He flexed shoulder muscles, had Isiga loosen the bindings about the upper part of his body, ready for any action he must take.

At a trilling cry from the outside, Isiga looked around.

"They come, Zannah says."

But Rees did not need the small Salarika's warning. The smell was enough—sickeningly heavy. Yes, Crocs were on the march.

"Get to the robo landing, keep under cover!" He gave her the blaster and picked up his own weapons, if one could call a sleek coil of hagger hide rope a weapon.

Isiga dodged out the door, caught Zannah's hand and ran. But Rees' path led him towards the gate. He had earlier marked down his post there and he reached it now after a zig-zag route. So he crouched at last between two of the supporters of the flood nearest the barrier. Crocs would head for that, to douse the light, as soon as they were through the gate.

Hooting—harsh barking. The Ishkurians were certainly making no effort to hide their presence outside, attempting no sneak attack. They must know how few and weak their quarry were. And here they came!

A brown plated head, revealed in detail in the light, raised a snout pointing at the gate as might a hound what had treed a quarry. And, riding on the Ishkurian's shoulders, Gordy! Rees' heart gave a lurch of relief. The child was still unharmed!

The Croc's scaled hands went up, he stopped a trifle to allow Gordy to slide from his plate ridged back. Rees' breath came out in a hiss close to Isiga's expression of anger. That was Ishbi from the mission. No wonder Gordy had accepted such an escort readily. The native whom the boy had known as a friend for at least half of his short life, Ishbi who was a link with his home and family, Ishbi whom Gordy would now trust sooner than he might Rees himself.

Gordy walked forward confidently. He paused by the gate to look back and Rees saw Ishbi's head jerk in a movement approximating a Terran nod of encouragement. Other Crocs emerged into the open behind Ishbi, a wedge of them carrying some burden. Gordy was to open the gate and they would insert a prop to keep it so until they could all pour in. Simple, neat, and it would work. Ishbi had enough familiarity with the mission installations to head straight for the power and shut off all controls there.

The door in the larger barrier opened and Gordy walked bodly through. A concentrated rush from the wedge of hovering Crocs sent a log crashing into that opening. Now Ishbi, holding two giant slabs of taluc bark on either arm, took a running leap, skimmed along the log. The taluc bark smoked and the native threw them from him as he hit the inner side of the fortress wall. There were others coming the same path with their temporary shields covering them for that instant when they must pass the portal and cut the protecting ray operating there.

With the log providing them passage over the ground wire and the improvised shields, swift and daring runners could make the passage. However, they were not all to be so lucky as Ishbi and his first follower. The third native to make the jump gave a snorting cry as a convulsive leap took him through, only to lie writhing on the ground. There was a halt in the advance. Ishbi barked an order and turned to Gordy.

But the child was staring wide-eyed at the dying Croc. With a cry he began to back away. Ishbi made a grab for him and Gordy, looking up, must have seen something in the suarian countenance looming above him which was utterly disillusioning. He backed farther, his hands raised as if to fend off the big Ishkurian.

Rees went into action. The rope snaked out in a loop which encircled Gordy and pulled tight. Rees jerked, the distance between them was short enough so that the boy would not be hurt and it was the only way to get him quickly out of Croc clutches.

Gordy screamed, high and shrill, and Rees hauled him in. He held Gordy, rope and all, before the surprised natives were fully aware the Terran boy was out of reach. Gordy, his arms still pinned to his sides by the loop, fought and kicked in Rees' hold, but he was too hampered to break loose.

This was the worst, the dart and dash the Terran must make into the shadow of the nearest building, with two Crocs loose and perhaps more ready to attempt crossing the log bridge now that they were inflamed by seeing their prey directly in view.

Rees cringed within the wrapping bandages as he sped, expecting at any moment as he held to that zig-zag path to feel the bite of an Ishkurian dark in his back. Perhaps it was his weird appearance in that purple covering which gave him a few seconds grace when the Crocs sighted him. If they were expecting a Terran or Salarika to show, then a purple thing of totally alien species would be momentarily startling. And the majority of Crocs were not quick thinkers.

Even so Rees was hardly able to believe he had actually made his first run without opposition when he crouched in the door of the com unit building, Gordy still wriggling and screaming wildly in his hold.

"Gordy!" The young man put his face closer

to the boy's, hoping that the sound of a familiar voice, a chance to see his features through that opening in the head bandages would prove his identity. "Gordy, it's Rees, Rees Naper!"

But Gordy had past the point where reason could appeal to his mind, he was completely hysterical. Holding him tight, Rees steadied for another rush. Ishbi leading that invading party was bad luck. The Ishkurian could recognize the guide beam, turn it off and ground the robo. Yet Rees could make no stand here, not with Gordy so wild and without a weapon.

He reached around, pressing the struggling child tight to his chest, and caught up the waiting blanket he had left there. That was also wringing wet with Isiga's preparation. Gordy gave a gasp as Rees wrapped the clammy folds about him, then subsided into a limp weight. Once more Rees broke into the open.

There was a crack behind him and the flood by the gate went out, shattered by some well flung dart. But the ensuing dark was an aid to the Terran now, not a danger. He ran for the 'copter park. Fire, a green-yellow fire ran along the ground there, stiffened into a four walled square of odorous flame. Rees marked the narrow gap before him, knew he must risk the tongues licking out on either side. He measured the distance ahead, put his face down against the bundle which was Gordy, and ran at the best speed he could muster for that slit passage to safety.

Heat scorched his hands, face. Rees raised his head. Isiga crouched in the square, the blaster barrel steadied on her forearm laid across her knee. Rees dropped Gordy, grabbed for the weapon.

"Have—to—get—back," he told her in labored gasps, "must—smash—beam—control."

Her ears were flattened, her lips curled in a cat's snarl of spitting rage. He caught the blaster as she released it. Already the flames from the oganna leaves were fifteen or more feet high, their heat spreading inward. With his palm Rees pushed the Salarika away from him toward the middle of the square. She pulled at Gordy and obeyed Rees' gesture, while the Terran turned again to face the gap, hardly sure now where the opening was.

One arm over his face, the other holding the blaster as tightly as he had Gordy, Rees set himself for another dash. The three would huddle down in the open, covered by wet blankets, hope that the robo would come in before the fire died. If he could reach the beam and render it safe from interference, a danger she should have foreseen.

Rees leaped, cried out as he met fire. Then was

beyond its breath. His bandages were no longer so wet. A charred strip fluttered free from his waist as he ran.

There ahead a shape moved, shadow against shadow. Rees fired with the blaster ray set on a wide fan, was answered by a hoarse croaking cry. Now he was in the control room, the light on as he had left it. But a brown serrated back, a snouted head, were between him and the panel. Once again the Terran fired, saw flame crisp across the Ishkurian, go on to cut the panel in two. The light in the room crackled and went out. Only the flickering dance of the burning oganna leaves gave any radiance. He had finished the main power set.

But the robo guide beam was equipped with a secondary impulse. And it would continue on that emergency changeover for at least an hour. Time and the duration of the storm would battle for their future. Rees had done all he could to safeguard their one slender hope. It remained for him now to try to save himself. With all controls off the Crocs would stream through the gate un-challenged. But they could not cross that flame wall, not until it smoldered into ashes. And ogan-na had a long burning period.

Rees slipped away from the control room. The smell of the burning leaves was heavy and aromatic, removing one of his safeguards, the ability to scent the enemy. Croc cries were harsh in the night and then, as if by command, they were suddenly stilled. He thought the natives were combing the buildings, circling that core of flame, attempting to herd their prey inward.

But the Terran still held one advantage, the ability to cross the fire wall, or so he hoped. Hurriedly Rees ran his hand down his body. Those protecting bandages had dried, but they still covered him. And he had no choice, he had to pass the gap for the third time. Death that way, painful as it was, would be better than any the Crocs would deal out to a prisoner.

Now to locate the gap once again. These waves of flame were confusing, and the slit had been a narrow one even in the beginning. To choose the wrong place meant complete disaster.

Behind Rees there was a noise, a guttural grunt. He fired at the sound and ran. Once more he flung his arm up to shield his face as he took off in a leap designed to carry him through the spot he believed was the thinnest in the wall of fire.

Then he was rolling over and over, his bandages smoldering in half a dozen places. When he was really aware of anything beyond the pain and heat, he knew that he was lying flat, most of his body bare as Isiga worked feverishly to tear those charred strips from him. Burns smarted, but he must have been lucky, very lucky.

"Can you move?" The Salarika bent over him to ask. "We must get back out of range."

Rees turned his head and saw what she meant. Darts were arching through the flames, catching fire in the process, to rain down on the pavement of the park. He rolled over and tried to creep out of range, but the pain in his hands, under the pressure of his weight, was too great for him to stand. Somehow Rees got to his feet, leaned heavily on Isiga as she towed him to the blanket heap which was the children. There she pushed him down and held a canteen to his lips while he drank greedily.

"Listen!" Her head went up, ears aprick. Now he could hear it too, the warning landing whistle of the Robo coming in to set down. They caught the green wink of its lights as the flyer made its verticle descent. Rees stood blinking as the tripod feet of the cabin touched the pavement. He wavered forward with an outstretched hand, and then moaned with pain as his seared fingers proved that that vision was indeed real, that they had beaten the nightmare after all.

Seconds later he waved Isiga into the pilot's seat, saw the children huddled behind her.

"They'll have her on robo-beam in reverse," he

said. "Use the lift button, and then the all-clear so the beam can pick us up."

Rees pointed out the proper controls, his hands so painful with the slightest movement that he had to grit his teeth against crying out. But in spite of that torment he smiled weakly as they rose straight out of the hollow of flame into the clean, cool air of the night. The spider had woven webs and caught victims, but not all, not all!

There was going to be a future in Nagassara or off world for them after all. Isiga's hands dropped from the controls as the robo pilot took over smoothly. She leaned toward the Terran, concern in her cats' eyes. But Rees continued to smile as they rode out on the beam lifting to the mountain pass where the day and the future were arriving close upon one another.